Praise for Half a Chance

★ "Lord has combined vivid, cinematic description with deft characterization and handles several important issues with sensitivity, nuance, and great skill. . . . A deeply enjoyable read."
— *School Library Journal*, starred review

★ "Lord offers a tender treatment of early adolescent needs and struggles in this thoughtful coming-of-age novel. . . . With subtle but effective imagery and a relatable protagonist, the title speaks to both human loneliness generally and the plight of a young girl in need of friendship."
— *Bulletin of the Center for Children's Books*, starred review

★ "With winning results, Lord brings the same sensitivity to the subject of dementia that she brought to autism in her Newbery Honor book, *Rules*."
— *Kirkus Reviews*, starred review

Also by Cynthia Lord

Rules
Touch Blue
A Handful of Stars

Shelter Pet Squad #1: *Jelly Bean*
Shelter Pet Squad #2: *Merlin*
Shelter Pet Squad #3: *Paloma*

Hot Rod Hamster
Happy Birthday, Hamster
Hot Rod Hamster: Monster Truck Mania!
Hot Rod Hamster and the Wacky Whatever Race!
Hot Rod Hamster and the Awesome ATV Adventure!
Hot Rod Hamster and the Haunted Halloween Party!
Hot Rod Hamster Meets His Match!

half a chance

CYNTHIA LORD

SCHOLASTIC INC.

Copyright © 2014 by Cynthia Lord

This book was originally published in hardcover by Scholastic Press in 2014.

ISBN 978-0-545-03534-7

10 9 8 7 6 5 4 3 2 1   16 17 18 19 20

Printed in the U.S.A.   40

First printing 2016

The text type was set in Janson Text.

Book design by Nina Goffi

To Robin

1

Out of Place

"Lucy, we're going to love this place!" Dad called to me from the porch of the faded, red-shingled cottage with white trim. "We can hang a swing right here and watch the sunset over the lake. And these country roads will be great for biking."

While my little dog, Ansel, explored some ferns, I took a deep smell of the pine trees lining the dirt driveway.

"I'll buy you a new bike when I get back, Lucy. Would you like that?" Dad asked.

"Maybe we can get *two* bikes," I yelled to him. "So we can ride together."

"Great idea!"

Dad always promises me things before he leaves and then forgets by the time he's home again. But I couldn't help having that little bit of "I hope so" that this place would be different. That's the thing with new beginnings — sometimes, they're more than just starting over again.

Sometimes they change things.

"There are more boxes in the van," Mom said, carrying a laundry basket full of kitchen stuff past me and across the flagstones leading up to the front porch steps.

"I'll get them in a minute," I promised. "Ansel needs to stretch." But really, I wanted to take my first New Hampshire photo before I went inside and everything got busy. Whenever we move, I take a picture as soon as we arrive. It always makes me feel a little braver, knowing that on some future day I can look back at that photo, taken when it was new and scary, and think, *I made it*. Like creating a memory in reverse.

On the drive from Massachusetts to New Hampshire, I'd been thinking about what my first photo would be. When Dad said he'd found us "a lovely red cottage on a lake," it sounded fancy.

Dad always says that red is a great color in a photograph, so I thought for sure I'd take a picture of our new house. But this washed-out red seemed to disappear into the woods behind it. The gambrel roof and two long windows above the porch made it look like an old barn with white-rimmed, tired eyes watching the lake.

This house didn't look like it was supposed to be quirky, though. It looked like whoever built it didn't really know how.

So I turned to see what the house was looking at: the bright blue lake, puckered by darker waves, and the four mountains — three graceful curves and one sharp peak — rising above the pine trees across the water.

When we lived in Vermont three years ago, there were mountains, too, but this would be my first time living on a lake. "Let's go down to the beach," I said, but Ansel pulled backward on his leash. "It's okay. You don't have to go swimming. We'll just look at the water."

Ansel's only fifteen pounds, but those fifteen can feel like a hundred when I'm tugging him to come and he's pulling back: *No way.*

I had to carry him. Between the lawn and the lake were thousands of smooth, soft-colored rocks: white,

3

gray, rust, yellow, and tan. They crunched under my feet, sounding like marbles rubbing together or Scrabble pieces as you mix them up. *Flip-flops are the wrong shoes for this*, I thought as my foot slid to the side.

Ansel's nose twitched at the unfamiliar lake smell: weedy and a tiny bit fishy. Out in the middle, the water was sparkling-pretty, like someone had spilled a whole bottle of glitter out there. But up close, an icky border of bright yellow pollen floated along the lake's edge. Beyond the pollen, a school of tiny minnows swam along, shifting directions quickly. *This way! No, that way! Who's in charge here?*

When I set Ansel on the sand, he immediately leaned down to sniff a little brown moth that was stuck in the pollen, fluttering. The moth might already be too wet, too exhausted to live. But I found a leaf to scoop him out of the water and placed him gently on a rock so he could dry his wings.

Even half a chance beats none.

Holding my camera to my eye, I saw I had ruined my shot. Now the colors were too close: drab brown moth on drab brown rock. And there was no story. It was just a moth stuck to a rock.

Dad would've thought of the photo first. He would've shot the moth struggling in the pollen and found a way to make people care — even though it was just a plain, ordinary, dying bug. Dad's an amazing photographer, and he says it's just as important to show the hard things in the world as it is to show the beautiful ones. Even in the midst of horrible things, there are little bits of wonder, and all of it's true.

Ansel barked. Switching off my camera, I glanced where his nose pointed. On the beach next door was a row of kayaks, and an older lady was standing on the dock. Sitting next to her were a boy and a girl, both about my age, with their feet in the water and towels draped around their shoulders. Smaller kids were swimming nearby, just their heads showing above the waves. "Grandma Lilah, watch me!" a small voice yelled. "I'm a water bug!"

Ansel barked again. "Hush," I told him. "Don't bark at our neighbors. They live here."

The gray-shingled cottage next door looked how I had imagined a cottage on the lake would look: a fairy-tale house with bright-white painted lattice crisscrossing the tops of the bow windows and dormers jutting out from the roof. Baskets of red petunias hung on the long front porch.

Beside it, our cottage looked like a run-down summer camp on move-in day, with random boxes and suitcases and stuff in the yard.

Watching the neighbors having fun together at their pretty house made me feel lonely, not just alone. At twelve years old, I'd already moved three times in my life. I should've been able to march over there and say: "Hi, I'm Lucy. We just moved in," and not be scared. Practice only made it familiar, though. Never easy.

Ansel barked again, and the boy on the dock looked over at us.

Uh-oh! I lifted my hand and swished it by my ear, so it could go either way: waving if he was friendly or brushing away a mosquito if he wasn't.

The boy waved back, got to his feet, and started walking down his dock toward the beach.

Is he coming over here? I took a deep breath. Dad had driven us past my new school, and it was so small that any new girl would stick out immediately in September. It would really help if I made some friends over the summer.

I gave the boy my warmest smile. "I'm Lucy, and this is Ansel. We just moved in."

"I'm Nate." As he reached out his hand to Ansel, I gripped the leash. Ansel doesn't love everybody.

"We're sooo glad to meet you!" I said, in my sweetest, most singsongy voice, so Ansel would hear the "happy" in my voice and feel okay about the hand coming toward him. He took a glancing sniff of Nate's fingers. His ears, which usually stuck up, stayed back, but the tip of his tail wagged.

Nate smiled, the freckles rising across his nose. There was a slight gap between his front teeth, which made his face interesting and a little funny and quirky — a *good* quirky. I couldn't believe how comfortable Nate seemed only wearing shorts and a towel. I'd be cringing if I had to meet someone in my bathing suit.

"We noticed the FOR SALE sign was gone," Nate said. "We were wondering who would be moving in."

"It's us," I said, and immediately wished I'd said something smarter. Of course it was us! "Though my dad leaves tomorrow on a trip to Arizona for his work, so it'll be mostly me and my mom this summer."

Ansel barked again, and I noticed the girl from the dock was coming up the beach, too. She wore glasses, and her long hair hung in wet pigtails.

"Lucy, this is Megan," Nate said. "Her cottage is the yellow one down at the point."

"Hi." I gave her a bright smile.

Megan tipped her head a little sideways, looking at me over her glasses. "How long are you here for?" she asked.

"We're going to live here," I said simply.

"Cool," Nate said, grinning. "My grandma owns our cottage. We live in New Jersey, and my family usually only comes for two weeks, but this year we'll probably be here all summer!"

"I always come for the whole summer," Megan said. "I know just about everyone on the lake — at least on our side. Our real house is in Connecticut."

Neither of them went to school here. I froze my mouth in a smile so my disappointment wouldn't show.

"Come on, Nate," Megan said. "We're supposed to be helping Grandma Lilah watch the little kids while they're swimming."

"Do you want to come over, Lucy?" Nate asked.

"We just got here," I said. "I need to help unpack."

"Okay. See you later," Megan said.

Watching them walk away, I wondered if maybe I should've gone. Even if Nate and Megan didn't go to school here, a summer friend would make things better *now*. And most times, kids decide if they're going to like you really fast. Saying no might've blown my chances.

One thing I'd learned about moving was that once you were there, it was better to just look ahead. Because even if you went back to visit the places and people you left behind, it was never the same —

except in photos. Those always keep everything exactly the way it was: a sharp-steepled white church against thunderclouds near our old house in Vermont, rainbow-colored graffiti on the overpass near our apartment in Boston, yellow window light slanting out across the wet cobblestones near our rented rooms on Nantucket.

I pointed my camera straight down and took a photo of my feet in my flip-flops on the shore with my toes almost touching the rim of yellow pollen.

New Hampshire: Day One.

2

A New Day

Before dawn, I woke to an eerie wavering cry, wild and lonely.

For a moment, I panicked, not even remembering where I was. Then, with a big "oh, yeah," it all came back: New Hampshire, our tired-looking house, the lake, Nate who seemed friendly and Megan who didn't. Today, Mom and I would be driving Dad to the airport for his trip.

In the damp almost-morning, even the dark felt like someone else's. On top of the covers, Ansel let out a low growl. "Shh," I said, reaching down to pat his back. "It's okay. Whatever is making that weird sound is staying outdoors."

Mom hadn't wanted a dog, but a few months ago, Dad had returned from a photography trip to Montana holding a dog carrier. Peeking out of the front was a scruffy, mixed-breed, black-and-white dog. "Meet Ansel," Dad had said, naming the dog for Ansel Adams, a famous photographer who had shot beautiful black-and-white photos. Mom said our landlord would have a fit, but Dad said Ansel was a stray and all alone, and Dad couldn't leave him that way. "Somehow, it'll work out," he said.

Here's how it worked out: The landlord told us to leave.

Dad probably wouldn't admit it, but I think he was relieved. He craves moving the way other people crave staying put. After we move he's fine for a while, but then he starts looking at maps and websites. "I've taken all the photos I can of this place," he'll say.

But really, I think Dad loves how good it feels to leave — to let go of the routine in an old place and start over somewhere else.

The mournful sound came from outside again. I shivered, climbing out of bed to shut the window. The lake was an open, lapping darkness except for shifting speckles of moonlight on the surface.

Below, on our beach, I could make out Dad with his tripod.

I ran my hand over the wall beside the door frame, feeling for the light switch so I could get dressed and find my camera on the old wooden bureau some previous owner hadn't wanted to take with them. Everything creaked: the wide floorboards, my room's antique brass doorknob, and the heavy, white-painted door. "I'll be back," I whispered to Ansel.

By the time I got to the beach, the sky already glowed dusty blue. "Hey, Lucy. I hope I didn't wake you," Dad said. "I thought I'd shoot our first New Hampshire sunrise."

"Me, too." The early morning was so quiet that I could hear the waves hitting the beach, the leaves moving, and the birds chittering. From somewhere far away, a train whistle blew.

Across the water came that haunting call again. "What's that sound?" I asked. "It sounds like a wolf howling!"

"That's the loons," Dad said. "They're black-and-white waterbirds, a little bigger than a duck and a bit smaller than a goose."

"*Birds* are making that sound?" I asked. "Are they going to do that *every* morning?"

He smiled. "Probably. But they'll only wake you up this time of year. They come to the lakes in the spring to fish and raise their chicks. But in October or November, they'll leave to spend the winter on the ocean. Really, we're lucky to have them — they are a threatened species in New Hampshire."

"I bet it's their neighbors who are threatening them!" I joked. "Because they're annoyed to be woken up." I felt a tiny jab on my neck and slapped at the mosquito. Where there was one, there were sure to be a hundred more coming. "Do you want some bug spray?" I asked.

Dad didn't look up from his camera, so I dug around in his backpack until I found it. I don't like the sticky, tight feeling of bug spray on my skin, but bug bites are worse.

As pink blushed the horizon, I looked for a good subject for my shot. No need to think about the background — that'd be the lake and the morning sky. But I needed something for the foreground. The left-behind lawn chair on Nate's dock might make a pretty black silhouette. But I'd have to walk on their beach to get a good shot. "Do people own the beach? Or just their lawn?"

"I don't know," Dad said. "But it doesn't matter. We're the only ones awake this early."

The surrounding cottage windows were all dark. Maybe Dad was right and no one would know. As the sky was deepening into mauve and blue, I hurried to find a spot on the sand near Nate's family's dock.

"Here it comes!" Dad called.

A streak of sun surged over the mountains on the far side of the lake. I shot and shot, trying different angles and positions of the chair against the sky.

Dad took a few pictures and then quickly moved his tripod to a different place. Sunrise and sunset give some of the best light all day: warm and golden. But it comes and goes like *that*.

We were shooting the same sky, but I already knew his photos would be better. For one thing, he had a fancier camera. Mine was just a point-and-shoot camera with some extra settings and a bigger, better lens than most. But it wasn't just his expensive camera or the fact that Dad had more experience that made the difference. You could call it having "a good eye" or talent, but it's what adds the spark. And whatever you call it, Dad has it.

The sky was light blue now, but the clouds were sugary pink.

"Isn't it something?" Dad said.

The black jagged line of pine and spruce treetops across the lake made a nice contrast against the pink and orange clouds. But when I turned on the camera's LCD screen and looked at my photos, none of them captured how beautiful it was in real life. None were good enough to impress Dad.

When the sun was a hot ball above the trees, we turned to see what the sunlight was slanting across to touch.

"Those three kayaks on the beach will make a good shot." Dad nodded at a row of overturned kayaks on Nate's beach. "From the dock, I can get a good, clean background."

It might be iffy who owned the sand, but there was no question who owned the dock — not us. What if someone at Nate's house looked out the window and saw Dad and thought we were pushy people who didn't care about what was ours and what wasn't? The wooden planks squeaked with his footsteps. But no one came running out of the house to tell us to go away, so I knelt beside the bushes at the edge of the lawn.

Sometimes you miss little things when you stand over them and look down. Sure enough, strung among the leaves of a blueberry bush was a perfect, teeny spiderweb, shining with beads of dew. At the bottom of the web was a fat black spider. I tried so many angles of that web that my knees hurt from kneeling so long. I clicked on the camera's screen to see my shots. A close-up picture is like entering another world where little things are gigantic. I scrolled through to find my best spiderweb photo.

As I walked over to Dad, I was excited to show him something he hadn't seen. "Not bad!" he said as we looked at it together. "See how the light is hitting every strand? It doesn't even have a good background, but the light on the waterdrops shows it off beautifully."

"I found it, though," I said under my breath, annoyed that he had given all the credit to the light.

"Hello," someone called.

My heart jumped to see the old lady from next door in her yard. "Are you going out to see the loons?" she asked.

"Your kayaks look so beautiful in the morning light," Dad said. "I was taking a photo of them. Would you like to see?" Mom always says Dad has a way with people. He just smiles and starts talking and people love him. I wish he'd passed that way on to me. It'd be a whole lot more useful than just giving me his stick-straight brown hair and his blue eyes.

He walked up on her lawn to show the woman the photo on his camera's screen. "I'm Dan Emery, and this is my daughter, Lucy. We've just moved in next door."

"You can call me Grandma Lilah. Everyone does." She smiled as the loon wailed again. "The loons have a nest on a little island across the lake. Some years they lay just one egg and other years they lay two."

Dad fidgeted with his camera, and I knew he was fretting that the light was going fast. "That's wonderful. Lucy, maybe you can take some photos of the loons to show me when I get home?"

"Sure," I said. "If they let me get close enough."

"Be here at ten o'clock," Grandma Lilah said to me. "That's when we do Loon Patrol."

I drew in a sharp breath. Did she think I was asking to go with them? "Oh, I didn't mean —"

"Can you swim?" she asked. "You don't usually have to, but if the kayak tips over, it's good to know how."

If the kayak tips over? "I've never been kayaking."

"It's much easier than canoeing," Dad said. "But Mom's driving me to the airport around ten. You'd miss coming with us."

I opened my mouth, but I felt both ways. I wanted to spend as much time with Dad as I could. But he's always full of details for his trip right before he leaves on a long photography assignment. And airport good-byes are the saddest, emptiest good-byes when you're the one staying behind. I hate that moment when

Dad walks off to security and then looks back and gives one last wave. Though he tries to hide it, I can tell he's excited to be heading off somewhere new. I don't say it, but I always wonder, *What if he doesn't come back? What if this time he's unlucky and gets some weird flu or is bitten by some poisonous animal, and that excited, happy-to-be-leaving wave is the last thing I see?*

But if I said no to our new neighbors again, they might stop asking me. Dad was going to Arizona, and I had to make it work *here*.

I threw Dad an apologetic glance. "Would it really be okay if I don't come to the airport?"

He frowned a little, but nodded. Turning to Grandma Lilah, he said, "You'll watch out for Lucy if we let her stay behind?"

"Of course!" she said, smiling.

The light in the sky had turned to white — a colder light now. As Dad and I walked home toward our cottage, I hoped I hadn't hurt his feelings.

"I got some nice shots," he said. "Nothing great, but they're okay. Are you hungry? I'll see if I can figure out the stove and make us some breakfast before I have to get packing."

"I wish you didn't have to go *today*," I said.

"Me, too," Dad replied. "But you can text me and call me."

"Don't worry, I will!" I'd been begging for my own phone ever since some other kids at school started getting them. Mom and Dad's answer was always no, until a few weeks ago when it turned to yes. I think maybe the phone was an apology present for moving again.

"Texting will be easier than calling," Dad said. "There's the time difference between New Hampshire and Arizona, and sometimes I'll be too busy to answer a phone."

"Okay," I said.

Our footsteps crunched the little beach rocks, sounding extra loud in the quiet around us.

"You know it's hard for me to go, right?" Dad asked. "But it's my job and it's important. It's only for a while, and then I'll be home for a much longer stretch."

As much as I hated for him to go, I did understand. When I'm thinking about how to frame a shot and when to click, there's nothing else. It fills me up in a good way. And Dad doesn't just take pictures, he tells stories with his photos: a tiny animal that's almost extinct, people who don't get along with each other, or harsh remote places that most people would never get to see if he didn't show them.

Still, I wish he could do that important, make-a-difference thing at home. Most times when one of the magazines he works for sends him on a trip, he's only gone for a week or so. But every now and then, it's for many weeks. This time was one of the longest — almost two months. And he was leaving us behind to do all the work of moving. "It's just how it all worked out this time," he said, but I couldn't help thinking it had worked out better for him than for us.

"Look," Dad said. "There's a loon flying. It must be the mate, called home by the one we've been hearing."

The bird flying over the lake was big, but not soaring gracefully like an eagle or a hawk. He was beating his wings fast, like it was a struggle to stay in the air. He landed with a long splashdown on the water.

"Good morning!" I heard behind me.

I looked back to Grandma Lilah standing alone on her dock, but she wasn't talking to us. She was looking out at the lake, calling to the loons.

Skip

As Dad packed and Mom unpacked in the living room, I checked the clock every few minutes so I wouldn't miss ten o'clock, when I'd promised Grandma Lilah I'd be ready for kayaking and Loon Patrol (whatever that was).

Why did I agree to try something *new* with people I didn't know? What if I fell in the lake?

"I can't take any more to Arizona than I have to." Dad looked around the living room at the piles of equipment and clothes. "Some of these planes are so small, the pilots even wanted to know how much *I* weigh."

"But they're safe?" Mom asked, pulling books from one of our moving boxes.

"Don't worry," Dad said. "These pilots have been flying these routes forever. I'll call when I get there — as long as I can get cell phone reception."

"Call me, too," I said. "Remember, I have my own phone now."

"Okay." Dad picked up a paper from his pile. "Oh, yeah. I forgot about this. Lucy, would you do me a favor? A bunch of portfolios will be coming in the mail from my editor sometime in August. Would you keep an eye out for them? It'll be a big package. Just put it somewhere that I can find it when I get home, okay?"

"All right," I said. "What kind of portfolios?"

"It's for a contest I'm judging. I told Marjorie I wouldn't have time, but she insisted. So I have to judge them as soon as I get home."

"Can I see?" I reached for the paper.

PHOTO SCAVENGER HUNT!

Kids, send us a CD that includes just one photo that best shows each of the following words or phrases. Be creative! Contest entries must be postmarked by **August 1.**

Your Name
Design
Three Feet
Secret
Collection
Skip
Holding On
Sticky
Journey
Beyond Reach
Heading Home
At the Shore
Exit
Left Behind
Lines
A Closer Look
Wonder
Unexpected
On Its Own
A New Day
At the Crossroads
Out of Place
Texture
Hope
Now and Then
Lost

Photos will be judged on technique and creativity by world-renowned nature photographer Dan Emery.

Why didn't he tell me about this?

As I folded the list small to fit in my shorts pocket with my camera, Ansel got up from his snoozing spot near the window and flopped down at my feet. He kept lying down and getting up and moving to a new spot — like he had to try them all to see which ones felt right.

"Hey, Ansel," I said. "Get the *leash*?"

Ansel's head snapped up. *Leash* is one of Ansel's tail-wagging words (*treat*, *car*, and *bacon* are others). It stung that Dad hadn't told me about the contest, and I didn't want to sit there and watch him pack.

When Ansel gets excited, he can't pick between running and jumping, so he does both. He ran-jumped around the room, messing up one of Dad's piles on his way.

I waited until we were outside and away from the living room windows before I looped Ansel's leash around my wrist and unfolded the contest paper.

Maybe Dad thought I wouldn't be interested? Or maybe he worried people would say I had an unfair advantage because he was the judge? But the uneasy feeling in my stomach was afraid it wasn't for either of those reasons. Maybe Dad hadn't told me because he thought I had no chance of winning.

As Ansel sniffed a clump of birch trees beside the driveway, I looked through the contest words. Some would be difficult, and others were full of possibilities. "Lines" could be people waiting for concert tickets, ripples moving outward in water, rows of bricks on a building, tree trunks.

I glanced up into the birch trees. The mix of light and shadows on the leaves created changing shapes and different greens. Leaves are brighter when they're lit from above. And the blue sky gave some nice contrast.

I turned the camera portrait-style. This photo was all about soaring height. I took baby steps until all the white birch trunks worked together in the frame, thick at the bottom, thinner as they climbed, ending in a burst of leaves, like fireworks exploding. Beautiful, strong *lines.*

As I clicked the shot, Ansel started wagging all over. When he makes a friend, he makes it hard.

"Hey, Lucy!" Nate said, coming across his yard like we'd been neighbors forever. "What are you doing?" He reached out to pat Ansel.

I glanced at the paper in my hand. "Oh. I just found out about a photography contest. It's like a scavenger hunt — except instead of collecting *things,* you take photos. I was playing around with one of the words." I flipped on my camera's screen and showed Nate my shot of the birch trees. "This is 'Lines.'"

"Wow, that's good! It looks like it could be a post-card," Nate said. "What do you get if you win?"

I hadn't even checked, so I scanned the rules at the bottom of the page. "First place gets five hundred dollars and all the winner's photos are published in the magazine. They also pick three runners-up, who each get two hundred fifty dollars and one photo published, and then there are some honorable mentions who just get their names printed."

Nate looked at the list with me. "This looks fun! 'At the shore' would be easy. You could just take a picture of the lake."

I looked over at the lake: sun reflecting off the waves, the mountains rising above the trees on the far side, and a sailboat in the middle. It was pretty, but ordinary. "It's a good idea, but I bet lots of kids' photos would look exactly like this. If I were *really* doing the contest, I'd want mine to be different, so it would stand out."

As soon as I said it, I worried I might've hurt Nate's feelings and wished I could take the words back.

But he grinned. "There's a dead fish down on the beach. That'd be different. And it's at the shore!"

I smiled with relief. "That'd be *too* different!"

"Can I help you look for something?" he offered. "I can't go home yet. One of my little cousins ate the other one's Popsicle. Now they're both crying. I came outside to escape."

I'd never had a boy as a good friend before. And I'd never had a friend who liked taking photos with me, either. "Sure," I said.

But as we headed for the lake, Ansel had other ideas. "He doesn't like water," I told Nate. Ansel licked my hand as I knotted his leash around a little tree growing at the start of the sand. "Okay, you win. You can stay here, but no barking, okay?"

At the shore, I crouched to examine the sand. From a distance, sand seems like one big thing, but up close, it's a million tiny ones. A carpet of baby rocks.

But the problem with sand is that it makes a better background than a subject for a photo. So I looked for something small to place on the sand. All I found were a few little sticks of driftwood, some pinecones, a dirty snarl of rope from someone's boat, and a cigarette butt.

"Nothing seems special enough," I said.

"How about a different word, then?" Nate said. "If you skipped a rock on the water, that could be 'skip.' It'd be a cool action shot."

"It'd be hard to skip a rock and hold the camera still enough to take the photo," I said. But really, I didn't know *how* to skip a rock, even though I'd tried tons of times before.

"I'll do it." Nate kicked off his sneakers. "We need some good flat rocks — the flatter, the better."

Underwater looked bumpy, and some of the rocks had a greenish slimy haze on them. So I kept my flip-flops on and stepped in. My bright pink nail polish and blue flip-flops stood out brilliantly against the green and tan and gray of the lake bottom. My teeth clenched with the cold, but the water felt soft around my ankles.

Nate's first rock sliced into a wave without bouncing once. "I have to throw them out farther," he said.

Holding tight to my camera with one hand, I reached down through the water with my other to help him find rocks. A wave splashed little pinpricks of cold drops up my bare arm. The first rock I chose looked flat from above, but when I pried it from the sand, the other side was rounded like the bottom of a bowl. I dropped it back. The next rock was flat and smooth.

Nate waited for me to get the camera ready before he threw. Six skips!

I could hardly click fast enough to keep up. "Wow! How'd you get so many?"

"The trick is to get low," Nate said. "If you throw higher, it doesn't work as well. And then put some spin on it — more spin, more skips." He picked up another rock. "You put one finger on top like this. Then twist the rock as you throw. I'll hold your camera, if you want to try."

"No, that's okay," I said quickly. "I'll take the photos."

I changed my setting to "burst" so my camera would take a whole series of shots with each click. Nate threw again. Just before I saw the rock in the frame, I pushed the button. Nate's next rock skipped five times and I got off a burst of shots.

"So where did you live before here?" he asked.

"Massachusetts, right near Boston," I said. "This is a big change."

"A good change? Or a bad change?"

I thought about it. "Both. Even though this town seems really small, I don't know where anything is yet. But there are some good things, too."

"Like what?"

I shrugged. "The lake is nice. I have a bigger room and it's on the corner of our house, so I get two windows instead of only one. I love animals, so I'm excited there are more of those here."

"I saw a moose last summer. He was over in the pond near the dump," Nate said.

"That's cool!" I said. "I didn't know there was a pond."

The water had been biting-cold, but I was surprised how fast I'd gotten used to it. Or maybe I was just numb now.

"I can help you find where things are," Nate said. "I've been coming here with my family ever since I was born. Do you have any brothers or sisters?"

"No, it's just me and my parents and Ansel." I glanced at Nate to see if he were hoping there was someone else he could be friends with, instead of me. But he didn't look disappointed.

Turning sideways, Nate tossed off a rock. "We have a houseful this summer: my grandmother, my parents, my older sister, Emily. She's fifteen. And my aunt Pat is here with Morgan and Mason, her two little kids. I like Morgan and Mason in small doses, but all summer is a *big* dose."

"Wow. That's a lot of people."

"It's *too* many people!"

I clicked as the next rock crashed into the water. "Sorry, that one stunk," Nate said.

I probably had a few good shots already, but I didn't want it to be over. We hunted rocks and Nate threw them, one after the other, until Ansel was asleep under the little tree and someone called, "Nate! Loon Patrol!"

"Do you think you got a good enough 'skip'?" he asked.

"I won't know until I look through them," I said. "But thanks! I have to bring Ansel back inside and say good-bye to my dad. Then I'll be ready for Loon Patrol."

"You're coming with us?" Nate asked, surprised.

My smile fell. "Grandma Lilah invited me. But I don't have to —"

"No, that's great!" Nate said quickly. "It's usually just Emily and me."

I swallowed hard. "I don't even know what to do on a loon patrol. And I've never kayaked before. I thought Grandma Lilah would show me."

He grinned. "Don't worry. It's easy. There's a group called the Loon Preservation Committee that keeps track of how the loons are doing in New Hampshire. So if you live on a lake, you can volunteer and tell them about your loons: how many you have and if they lay eggs and if they hatch — stuff like that. Grandma Lilah's been our lake's loon person ever since I was little. She's the one who started calling it Loon Patrol. But she can't get out on the lake anymore, so my family takes turns doing it for her. There's a form to fill out, but Emily and I will do that. You can just come with us. Do you need a life vest and stuff?"

"I need everything," I said.

"No problem. We have extra. I'll get you a life vest and a paddle and meet you on our dock."

My wet flip-flops squished over all those little beach rocks as I walked up to untangle Ansel's leash from the tree where I'd looped it and then from every bush that he'd wrapped himself around.

Climbing our porch steps, I turned on my camera's screen to see my "Skip" shots. Some were so bad that I deleted them immediately, but I had two really good ones. The first wasn't a great photograph, but it had Nate in it. And *he* looked great.

And the other was a rock caught in midair, water rising in an elegant crystal crown behind it.

A perfect skip.

4

Heading Home

Wading out to the pink kayak bobbing in the knee-high water next to the dock, I didn't think this looked easy at all.

"Maybe the loons have a baby now," Grandma Lilah said from the dock. "There was an egg!"

"There are *two* eggs this year," Emily said. "Last year the loons only laid one, but this year they have two." She smiled and I noticed a space between her front teeth, smaller than Nate's but there just the same.

I was glad for that little gap, because when I first saw her, I wasn't sure if Emily would be nice. She had dark blond hair, parted on the side, and looked like the kind of cool, older girl who is good at every sport and doesn't have to try hard to be pretty. Those girls don't usually talk to me — unless they have to.

But Emily had said, "Great!" when Nate told her I was coming, like she really meant it. And when Nate asked if we should invite Megan, Emily said, "Not today. There are only three kayaks and Lucy's our new neighbor. I want to get to know her, too," and I liked her even more.

"The loons have two eggs!" Grandma Lilah said. "How wonderful! Did you write that down?"

"Yes." Nate tipped the clipboard to show me the *Volunteer Casual Site Survey Form*. "We fill this out every time we check on the loons. The Loon Preservation Committee wants to know the weather and if the water was choppy or calm. Then we write down how many loons we saw and what they were doing."

"Every day," Grandma Lilah said. "We must check on them every day."

"Pretty much," Emily whispered to me.

"Write down the time you start," Grandma Lilah said.

"I know! I've filled out all the beginning stuff, like I always do." Nate looked a little annoyed as he handed Grandma Lilah the clipboard. "We'll tell you everything we saw when we get back." He picked up a long double-ended kayak paddle off the dock. "Okay, Lucy. Hop in. Then I'll give you the paddle and push you off."

Hop in? I ran my thumb over the corner of my camera. It'd be safer if I left it on the dock, but being level with the water might make for some awesome photos. It'd give a sense of being right there.

From across the lake came a throaty howl. "That's the loon's wail," Grandma Lilah said. "The first one calls, *'I'm here. Where are you?'* And the second answers, *'I'm here!'*"

"I heard that sound this morning," I said.

"Have you heard them tremolo?" Grandma Lilah asked. "They tremolo when they're threatened. Like *this*."

Nate looked horrified as his grandmother made a sound like a long wobbly laugh, but I grinned.

"Lucy, it's easiest if you straddle the kayak first," Emily said. "Watch me."

I'd given up on looking cool when I put on the fat orange life vest and slathered sunscreen all over my face, arms, and legs. But I didn't want to make a total fool of myself.

"Don't think about it," Emily said, throwing her

leg over her own kayak in the water. "You just have to do it. Grandma Lilah can hold your camera while you get in."

I handed my camera to Grandma Lilah. "I wish I could show you how," she said. "But if I sat down there, I could never get up! These knees don't work like they used to."

Lifting one leg slowly across the kayak to the water on the other side, I felt like I was climbing on a pink, wiggly horse.

"Now just *sit*," Emily said.

I landed inside with a thump, my knees sticking up and the kayak swaying scarily side to side. When it finally stopped jiggling, I lifted my legs, one at a time, out of the water and into the kayak.

Grandma Lilah handed me my camera, but I wasn't sure where to put it. So I tucked it down the front of my life vest.

"Getting in is the hard part." Nate held a paddle out to me. Then he gave me a big push. I clamped my teeth together, afraid it would be tippy.

As the kayak glided ahead, I let myself relax — a little. The lake was flat, with only the tiniest breeze creasing the surface. I watched Emily dipping her paddle, first on one side, and then the other.

Dip and pull. Other side. *Dip and pull.* The paddle

and the water made a soothing music together: *splish-splash, splish-splash*. I felt a shiver of excitement to feel the kayak cutting through the water, the whole lake open to me. The morning sun slanted gold, making the pink of my kayak stand out warm and vibrant against the dark blue water and green trees on the far side of the lake.

I imagined Dad beside me: "It's pretty," he'd say. "But pretty isn't enough for a great photograph. Show me why I care. What's the *story*?"

It was hard to balance the paddle across the front of the kayak and then hold still enough to keep everything in focus with the camera. As soon as I stopped, the kayak began turning gently to a different view, like it had its own plan. But I managed to get some shots with the nose of my kayak in the foreground and Nate's cottage in the background. The person viewing the photo would feel like they were paddling for home. That was the story. Heading home.

But Dad always says that what you choose to cut out of the frame is as important as what you leave in. So I tried a different story. I took a few strokes to be facing the woods and zoomed in tighter so there were only trees and no cottages, making the scene look wilder than it really was — like the viewer was completely alone, the only person in the whole world.

Nate and Emily were way ahead of me now, so I dropped my camera back inside my life vest and pulled hard on my paddle to catch up.

"Were you taking a photo for 'at the shore'?" Nate asked as I glided up beside him. "Lucy's doing a photo contest," he told Emily. "It's like a scavenger hunt, only instead of finding things, you take photos."

"No, but I got one of your cottage that might work for 'heading home,'" I said.

"So what would you buy with the prize money if you won?" Nate asked.

Should I tell him that Dad was the judge? That I couldn't really enter? Nate seemed to think it was fun taking photos with me. And if we weren't doing the contest, maybe we wouldn't have anything to do together. New friendships break pretty easily if something goes wrong at the beginning. "Maybe two new bikes," I said, pulling ahead. "So me and my dad could go riding together this fall."

"If I had five hundred dollars, I'd buy a swimming pool for my yard back home," Nate said, catching up to me. "And if there was any money left over, I'd buy all the pizza I could and invite my friends over."

"That sounds fun."

"You don't need a swimming pool," Nate said. "Because you'll have the lake all year round."

He sounded envious. "You know more about the lake than I do," I said. "We've lived lots of places, but this is my first time on a lake."

"You should have a photo of your first time kayaking," Emily said.

"Yeah, I'll take your picture," Nate said. "Hold your paddle out to me."

"No. That's okay," I said.

But he kept his hand out so I held my paddle toward him. He pulled us together close enough so I could pass him my camera.

For all the photos I take, I hated having mine taken. Still, it wasn't *too* hard to smile.

A woman waved to us as she paddled by in a light-blue kayak with a white bichon frise wearing a pink life jacket in the kayak with her. The dog looked so happy. It made me wish Ansel were tucked into my kayak with me. Except he'd probably tip us both over trying to get back to shore.

"Hi, Mrs. Rigby!" Emily called. "Hi, Zoe!"

"You should bring Ansel kayaking with us sometime." Nate matched his strokes to mine. "Wait! I have a great idea! If you won the contest, you could get Ansel a super-swanky doghouse."

I laughed. "Ansel would rather live with me. So it'd have to be a kid-and-dog house. But he'd like the super-swanky part."

"I wish *we* could have a dog," Nate said. "But my dad's allergic. Plus, my parents are both teachers, so no one's home all day to take care of it."

"What do your parents teach?" I dipped my paddle and pulled hard, trying to stay next to Nate and Emily.

"Mom teaches second grade, but my dad teaches science at the same middle school where I go." Nate rolled his eyes. "He'll be my teacher next year."

"It'll be awful, Nate!" Emily assured him. "You'll have to remember to call him Mr. Bailey in school. And when I had Dad for science, he was harder on me than anybody else! When you're out running errands with him, and he sees something related to what he's taught you, you'll have to hear about it, too!" She sat up extra straight and made her voice sound like a teacher's: "Look, Nate! Here is a great example of electromagnetism in action!"

Nate groaned.

Maybe having my dad at school every day would be too much of a good thing. But I couldn't help thinking Nate was lucky.

"What do your parents do, Lucy?" Emily asked.

"My mom's a computer programmer, but she has several clients and works mostly from home," I said. "And my dad, um, takes photos. Actually, he's on his way to Arizona today. There's some rare insect that needs protecting there and he's going to take photos of it for a conservation magazine."

"That's cool. Most people want to get rid of bugs, not save them," Nate said.

I smiled, glad he thought that was cool. "Dad always says if you can get people to care about the little things, they'll care about the big things, too."

As we glided along, people waved to us from their yards. I tried to wave back, but every time I stopped paddling, my kayak turned and I'd have to take an extra stroke to get going the right way again. A few cottages on, I saw Megan outside. I slowed down to wave, but she didn't. So I concentrated on making my strokes look good, like I knew what I was doing.

"Nate, what did you say to Megan? She looks mad," Emily said.

Nate waved to Megan. "I didn't say anything."

Maybe it was *me* that Megan was mad at. Because I was kayaking with her friends and she wasn't. I moved my thumb from one side of the paddle to the other. I could feel blisters coming. The front of my shoulders and my biceps felt sore, too, but I didn't want Megan to know I needed to stop and rest. *Dip and pull. Dip and pull.*

Far from shore, the water was dark blue and deep. I'd never been way out in the middle of a lake before, and I hadn't known we would go this far. It felt tingly to be way out in the middle — like I was somewhere people didn't really belong.

I was getting the hang of kayaking. Moving along felt effortless, like floating. Emily lifted her legs out and over the sides so her feet could dangle in the water. I managed to kick off my flip-flops and get one foot out. The water felt silky cold on the bottom of my foot. I slipped my other foot out and over the edge, too. As I paddled, the water slid along under my feet, like they were surfing over it.

Ahead in the cove on the other side of the lake, dragonflies zipped over the water, crisscrossing and weaving like tiny helicopters on a search-and-rescue mission. As we got closer to a group of little islands, something frilly brushed my toes and I pulled my feet back into the kayak. It was probably just a weed, but it still felt creepy to be touched by something I couldn't see.

"The loons always nest somewhere on these islands," Emily said. "It's great when we get a loon chick on the lake and he makes it. And it's even better when there are two."

"Last year, the loons only laid one egg, and it didn't hatch," Nate told me. "The Loon Preservation Committee sent someone to take the egg away to find out why it didn't develop. The person said they didn't always learn why, though. It just happens sometimes."

"It was horrible," Emily said. "When the guy took the egg, the loons called and called. Afterward, the female went back to the empty nest and lay there flat with her wings spread out."

"Grandma Lilah took it really hard," Nate said. "Mom will make us all go home if that happens again. If they don't hatch this year, maybe we should pretend they did."

"We can't lie to Grandma Lilah all summer," Emily said. "She'll figure it out when she looks through the binoculars and there are never any babies."

Dipping my paddle, I moved smoothly behind them, watching the little whirlpools formed by their strokes go past. On my next stroke, my paddle hit something soft. A sudden splash, and a loon surfaced right next to my kayak. He turned his head to look at me with his brick-red eye. He let out a piercing cry, filled with wildness.

He startled me so much I screamed and dropped my paddle. *Would he rush at me?*

Up close, he was bigger than I expected, magnificent and strange: a velvety black head, a sharp tapered bill, a band of white stripes around his neck, and a windowpane pattern on his wings — like he was dressed up for a fancy concert, wearing a striped necktie and checkered vest. The loon swam quickly away from me, his head turning side to side. I yanked my camera out of my life vest and started shooting without even taking a second to check my settings. My hands were trembling, but I clicked and clicked.

The loon rolled forward, diving under the water with barely a splash.

I couldn't move, not even to breathe. I should've tried putting the camera near the water! I just couldn't think fast enough.

"Wow," Nate said, handing me back my paddle. "He must not have looked before he headed for the surface. They don't usually come that close. You okay?"

I let my breath go. "I'm fine," I said, but it was bigger and more complicated than that. The loon had stared straight at me, and I had looked back. It was scary, but I wished with all my heart that he'd do it again.

"That was the male," Nate said. "Only the males yodel."

"Figures, huh, Lucy?" Emily said. "The *boys* are the loudmouths."

I scanned the water, watching for the loon to come up again. When he finally did, he was far, far away.

"Their nest is on that first tiny island," Emily said. "I can see the female on it. That must be why he was so upset."

Paddling closer, I could see a few scraps of land poking out of the water. A little breeze moved the grasses, and a nest of vegetation and bottom muck was piled near the small island's edge. On the heap, the white ball of the loon's chest showed up first, and then her black head above those spotted wings. "Wow, if I hadn't known where to look, I wouldn't have even seen her," I said.

"Loons can't really walk," Nate said. "Their legs are set too far back on their bodies — which is perfect for swimming but awful for walking. So they have to build their nests right at the edge."

I leaned over the front of my kayak to get nearer the water. I zoomed in as tight as my camera could go.

"I wish we could get closer," Nate said. "But we're not supposed to annoy her."

"Do you see any eggs?" Emily asked.

"What do they look like?" I asked.

"They're pretty big," Emily said. "Kind of a medium brown with dark speckles."

Through the lens, I watched the loon drop her head low over the edge of the nest, her bill almost touching the water. Her wing shuddered and she lifted it a little. Then a little more. On my fifth shot, I caught a glimpse of something between her and the nest. "I think so," I said, clicking another shot. "She looks mad, though."

"Let's go, then," Nate said.

On the way home, I let Nate and Emily get ahead of me. From this distance, our house looked tiny, but I could see the driveway was empty. Mom and Dad were on their way to the airport. I hadn't wanted to go with them, but now I wished I had.

I'd send Dad a text when I got home, wishing him a good trip and telling him about the loons. Maybe he'd get it before he got on the plane and could even text me back.

As I paddled, I heard the haunting wail behind me. *I'm here. Where are you?*

And a few seconds later, from another direction: *I'm here.*

5

At the Shore

"You wouldn't believe what happened!" Emily said as I followed her and Nate into the big front room of their cottage. "A loon almost tipped over Lucy's kayak!"

"Lucy of the Loons!" Grandma Lilah said from the couch.

I blushed, embarrassed that she said that in front of Nate's whole family. *Please don't let that nickname stick.*

"Lucy lives in the Alexanders' old house. She just moved in," Nate said to everyone.

"Hi." I nodded, the smile frozen on my face, as Nate introduced me. His mom smiled kindly at me. His dad nodded over his magazine: "Hello, Lucy." Aunt Pat, who looked younger than Nate's parents, waved to me as she talked on her cell phone. And his four-year-old twin cousins, Morgan and Mason, didn't even look up from the toy cars they were rolling along the rows of the big braided rug in front of the fireplace.

The room was covered in shiny, honey-colored pine boards: running across the ceiling, up and down the walls, and over the floor. It smelled slightly musty, a combination of old wood and wool blankets and bacon from breakfast. "What a nice cottage," I said, looking at the painted sign over the fireplace: WELCOME TO THE LAKE.

"Thank you, dear," Grandma Lilah said.

"How do you like New Hampshire, Lucy?" Mr. Bailey asked.

"It's good so far. We've only been here a day."

"Lucy, we must have you and your family over for a cookout some evening soon," Mrs. Bailey said.

They were being very nice to me, but I don't like being in the spotlight. It's horrible and itchy to stand in someone else's living room when you don't know everyone, but they all know each other. Emily had insisted that Grandma Lilah would want to see my photos of the loons, though.

"The female loon was on the nest," Emily said.

"We must record it on the survey," Grandma Lilah said. "Where's my pen?"

"Don't get up. I'll do it," Nate said. "Lucy, show her your photos."

Relieved to have something to do, I turned on my camera. "I don't know if you'll see much on my camera's little screen —"

"I'll get my laptop," Mr. Bailey said. "So we can make it bigger."

While we waited for him to come back, I fingered my camera. The only open space to sit down was on the couch next to Grandma Lilah, but that had been Mr. Bailey's spot.

Aunt Pat pulled her phone away from her ear. "Nate, Megan stopped by while you were out. Her family is going to the movies tonight in Conway and she invited you to join them. I said you'd call her."

"See? I told you Megan wasn't mad at me," Nate said to Emily.

"Well, she sure *looked* mad," Emily said.

Next to the couch was a bookshelf full of books and framed photos: a black-and-white wedding photo and another of the cottage being built. There was a group I didn't recognize posed on the cottage's front porch, and some newer pictures of birthday parties and graduations. At our house, when we hang photos on the walls, they're mostly of places Dad has been.

One of Grandma Lilah's photos had been taken on the summit of a mountain. I recognized a younger Grandma Lilah with a little boy. I stepped closer to look. "Is this you, Nate?"

"That was the first time Nate climbed Cherry Mountain," Grandma Lilah said. "I have lots of photos of Nate. He's been coming to the lake ever since he was born."

"Show her the photo of Nate swimming in his diaper," Emily said. "That's a good one."

Nate made a face at her.

"We climb Cherry Mountain every year," Grandma Lilah said.

"We haven't done it for a *few* years," Mrs. Bailey said. "It's not an easy climb."

"Nonsense," Grandma Lilah said. "We'll go tomorrow."

"The twins are too young," Aunt Pat said. "I'll have to stay here with them."

"Dad and I have Loon Patrol tomorrow," Emily said.

Grandma Lilah looked at me. "What do you think?"

The mountain in the photo looked like a real climb, not a little hill. And Grandma Lilah had said she had knee troubles when we were getting into the kayaks. How could she climb a mountain? Didn't the rest of the family see that? Or maybe I was wrong? "Where is Cherry Mountain?" I asked, to change the subject.

"It's the pointy mountain that you see across the lake," Emily said.

"Nine o'clock, then. It's best to get an early start," Grandma Lilah said. "Wear some good shoes. Do we have your phone number?"

"My phone number?"

"In case we need to confer on the weather."

When Mom had given me my cell phone, she said not to give out my phone number to strangers. But these were our next-door neighbors, so it was probably okay. I wrote my cell phone number on the edge of the loon survey form and let go a relieved breath when I saw Nate's dad coming with his laptop. I gave him my camera's memory card.

"Oh, how pretty!" Grandma Lilah said as the first photo came on the screen. "Birch trees!"

I blushed to see my "Lines" photo on the screen. "Wait, these are older photos! Let me scroll through to the photos of the loon." I didn't want them to see the photo I'd saved of Nate skipping rocks.

"Lucy's doing a photography contest," Nate said. "That's the photo for 'lines,' and our cottage might be 'heading home.' Show them your list, Lucy."

"It's just for fun, really."

But Mr. Bailey said he'd like to see, and Mrs. Bailey nodded. So I pulled the list out of my pocket and passed it around.

"These are wonderful photos, Lucy," Mrs. Bailey said as I showed them the photos I had taken of their cottage from the water.

I opened my mouth to tell her about Dad being a famous photographer, but I didn't want to share her praise or have to give it away to Dad. So I just smiled — until I saw the next photo. It was the photo Nate had taken of me in the kayak. I looked like some weird half-girl, half-boat creature with everything below my waist inside the kayak. I clicked past it immediately.

The first loon photo was a horribly blurry shot of the male. "I'm sorry. My hands were shaking," I said. "He scared me when he suddenly popped up."

The next one was in focus, but the loon's black head didn't stand out very well against the dark muddy greens of the pine and spruce trees reflected in the water.

With each photo, the loon was a little farther away. But as he got smaller in the frame, the water around him was only blue, setting off his coloring better. I clicked through a whole series of almost identical shots.

"He's grand, isn't he?" Grandma Lilah said.

"I love his stripes and checkered wings," Mr. Bailey said. "You wouldn't think such bold patterns would make for good camouflage, would you? But even the white on his breast has a purpose. It makes it harder for the fish to see him up on the surface. Loons are underwater predators, after all."

Emily shot me a look. "See, I told you, Lucy. We get science lessons all the time."

Mr. Bailey threw a magazine at her playfully. "Well, maybe if you remembered my lessons, I wouldn't have to keep giving them!"

I smiled, even though their happy teasing made my dad feel even more gone.

In the next photo, the female loon was on the nest. Surrounded by yellow-green grasses and weeds, she had her head tipped down to the side, so close to the water she was almost touching it, watching me with that ruby eye. There was intense emotion in the way she looked ready to come after me if I got one inch closer.

"Wow!" Mr. Bailey said. "That's an amazing photo. But it's obvious you kids were too close."

Nate was trying to explain how fast it all happened, but I couldn't take my eyes off the screen. The photo was in focus and had good contrast, but it was so much more than just grass and a bird. The loon's body language was full of feeling, and looking at it made me feel it, too. I wished I could show this photo to Dad and watch his face brighten with excitement. "Now there's a story, Lucy," he'd say.

"Don't you think so, Lucy?" Nate said.

"Huh?" I asked, tearing my eyes away from the screen.

"I said that would be a great photo for 'at the shore,'" Nate said. "You wanted something different, right? And it's definitely at the shore."

"Do you see the egg?" Grandma Lilah asked.

"No, but I did take a few more." I clicked ahead to the next shot. The loon had lifted her wing slightly. In the photo after that one, she had lifted it a little more. I'd been shooting so fast, it almost looked like animation as I scrolled through. In the last photo, the loon had shifted even more.

"Wait a minute. What's that?" Nate asked.

I clicked the magnifier to enlarge the image. A little black head looked out from under her wing.

"We have a chick!" Grandma Lilah yelled. "Nate!"

He grinned, hugging her from behind. "I know! I'll write it down."

That night, after a pizza takeout supper with Mom, the sky was so thick with clouds I couldn't even see the mountains on the other side of the lake — like they had simply vanished. In between unpacking boxes, I sent Dad text messages so he'd have lots to read from me as soon as he landed.

The Baileys next door are nice. There are lots of them!

I might go mountain climbing tomorrow.

Loon Patrol was fun. I didn't fall in the lake. But something touched me. Maybe a fish.

Part of me burned to send Dad the photo I'd taken of the loon on the nest, but I was afraid he'd just text back *Wow!* and that would be the end of it.

I miss you. Ansel says "Woof."

How are the rare bugs in AZ? The bugs in NH aren't rare at all.

Text me when you get this, OK? Even if you think I'm asleep.

The wind blowing through my open window felt wet and energizing, threatening a thunderstorm. I hoped Dad's plane was far away, and he was safely reading or chatting with the person in the airplane seat next to him.

Ansel paced around my room with his ears back. Sometimes I think he forgets that he has a home now and we'll take care of him, so he doesn't have to worry about storms. I hoped all the animals outside had found a safe place, too. I imagined the squirrels racing for their dreys, the chipmunks diving into their burrows, and the loon chick safe and dry under the adult's wing on the nest. But loons live so much in the water that maybe rain doesn't bother them.

I watched a car pull up next to the Baileys' cottage. The car's headlights lit up the rain as Nate dashed off the porch and into the backseat.

The not-so-nice part of me hoped the movie Megan had invited him to would be boring. But even as I thought that, I felt guilty. She hadn't done anything wrong. I just had the feeling she didn't like me.

The shade over my window slapped the screen. Heat lightning lit the sky, followed by a crash of thunder. Ansel ran under my bed.

"Hey, buddy." I got down on my hands and knees to look at him wedged between the boxes I'd stored down there. His eyes looked huge and he panted with his tongue out. "Are you hiding?" I asked. "It's okay. It'll be over soon. Come on out."

At my voice, his head moved slightly. I could see in his eyes how much he wanted to come to me, but being scared took everything he had.

I pulled boxes into the middle of my room until I could fit under the bed with Ansel. It had to be confusing for him to be in a new place with all these new smells and scary sounds. His whole world had turned upside down and he didn't even know why. I lay on my stomach with my legs out in the room but my head under the bed next to him. "It'll be okay." I reached across to run my hand over his shaking back.

But with each clap of thunder, Ansel cringed, his ears flattening against his head. I didn't know what to say, so I sang to him. First I tried "Row, Row, Row Your Boat," but Ansel doesn't like water. So I switched to "Bingo," except with his name.

There was a girl who had a dog, and Ansel was his name-o.
                    A-N-S-E-L,
                    A-N-S-E-L,
                    A-N-S-E-L,
        And Ansel was his name-o.

Every time I sang his name, Ansel slowed down his panting — until the next thunder boom.

"Lucy?"

I saw Mom's feet first. Then her knees as she knelt down. Finally her face looked under the bed. "I came in to tell you to shut your window. What are you doing?"

"Ansel's shaking like a washing machine." Thunder crashed again, and his whole body tensed. I covered his ears. "Shh."

I heard the window slide closed, then Mom lay down on the floor with us. As she rubbed Ansel's face, he licked her finger. "It's just thunder," she said.

The rain pattered like popcorn popping against the roof. "I sent Dad some texts, but he hasn't answered me yet. What do you think he's doing?" I asked.

Mom sighed. "He said he'd call when he was all settled. But it'll be late when he gets there, so probably we'll hear from him tomorrow before he heads off to see his first location. And then he'll be out in the middle of a field or standing in a stream, surrounded by mosquitoes. And not even noticing because he's totally wrapped up in taking photos or thinking about taking photos."

"I'm sure he notices the mosquitoes," I said. "But the photos are more important."

"Ah, well," said Mom. "That's why I'm glad I have an indoor job. I don't think I could ever forget about the mosquitoes. But Dad wouldn't do well with my life, either. He needs more than that."

He needs more than us, I added in my head. We lay on the floor listening to the rain until the thunder finally stopped and Ansel fell asleep against my arm.

6

Texture

The first thing I did when I woke up the next morning was to check my phone. I grinned to discover three texts from Dad.

I'm in AZ! Off to bed now, but I'm excited to see it all in the morning. I bet the sunrises are beautiful here.

Have fun mountain climbing today.

I miss you, too.

The texts made me feel a little better. I replied, even though he was probably still asleep.

Miss you more. Hope you get some great photos!

When Dad goes on a long trip, it's always hardest the first week. That's when I feel the hole of him being gone the worst — at every meal where his chair is empty, every bedtime when he doesn't say "good night." It's a sharp hurt, every day.

There's one good part about that first week, though. Mom and I do and eat all the things we both like but Dad doesn't.

"I was thinking maybe we could go out to lunch today?" Mom said during breakfast. "We could drive to North Conway and explore the shops there. The unpacking will still be here when we get back."

"That sounds fun. But could we do it another day?" I asked. "The Baileys invited me to go mountain climbing." I felt bad that she looked so disappointed. "I'm sorry, Mom. It all came up kind of fast. Do you want to come with us?"

"No, that's okay," she said. "I should keep unpacking. It'll be nice to feel more settled."

"We can go shopping in any weather," I said,

trying to make it seem less like I was choosing the Baileys over her. "And today's supposed to be nice out. But maybe you and I could have banana splits for supper? Like we did when Dad went to British Columbia last year? We got hot fudge sauce and whipped cream and everything. Remember?"

She smiled. "Yes, that would be fun! I'll go to the grocery store this afternoon and get everything we need."

When I'd woken up, I had wondered if climbing Cherry Mountain was just an idea or a real plan. But as I was getting dressed that morning, Nate texted me:

Do u have bug spray u can bring 4 r climb? We r out.

It was exciting to get a text from someone who wasn't my family. And who used funny text abbreviations. And was a boy.

Sure, I texted back, and then after I hit the SEND button, I wondered if that sounded blunt and maybe I should've used more words. So I sent another one. We have lots.

At nine o'clock, Nate was outside our door. I looked around him for the others, but it was only him.

"Is Grandma Lilah coming?" I asked.

He shook his head. "She couldn't walk that far, forget climbing. So I snuck out. I felt bad doing it, but she was in the kitchen talking to Emily about the baby loon. I don't think she even remembered about climbing."

"But it was her idea. Won't she be upset that we left without her?" It didn't seem right not to tell Grandma Lilah.

"She'll be *more* upset if she can't make it up the mountain," Nate said. "She gets mad when she thinks she can do something and we say it's not safe anymore. Or she tries and she can't do it. Honestly, she'll be happier at home hearing about the baby loon from Dad and Emily. Do you still want to go?"

I paused. "Okay, sure. If you do."

"Yeah. I was thinking maybe you could bring your camera and take some photos of our climb for Grandma Lilah? That way she'd get to see it, without having to do it herself," Nate said. "And maybe you'll even find some things to shoot for the contest? My mom said she'd drive us to the trailhead whenever we're ready."

As I followed Nate toward his family's van, I looked over at the beach and to Grandma Lilah standing on the dock with her clipboard. I still felt a little guilty. She had seemed so excited and happy last night, like she really wanted to go. "Nate, can you run in and grab that old photo of you and Grandma Lilah on the mountaintop? I have an idea."

He grinned when I told him my plan. "I'll be right back!"

The Cherry Mountain Trail began with an official-looking sign, but once Nate and I had walked several hundred feet, it became a green tunnel through the woods, the path nearly swallowed by ferns and trees. Every time I looked ahead and saw another fat yellow rectangle of paint someone had stroked onto a tree to mark the trail, I breathed out in relief.

Not lost yet.

The ground under my feet felt squishy from last night's rain, like walking on foam. My ears rang with the quiet of tiny sounds: a faraway bird cawing, the hum and buzz of insects, an occasional red squirrel pipping or moving about through the leaves. And my own breath as I climbed.

As we walked, I worried I was breathing too loud. Or talking too much. Or not enough. *Don't be dumb. It doesn't matter. He wouldn't have asked you to come if he didn't want to be friends.*

Maybe this was how it was supposed to feel when you had a boy as a friend? Part exciting and part weirdly confusing?

"I didn't realize it'd be so muddy," Nate said. "But I guess we did get a lot of rain last night."

"Yeah. Ansel was so scared of the thunder that he hid under my bed. I went under there with him."

Nate laughed. I wanted to ask him about the movie he went to see with Megan, but I really only wanted to hear that it was bad.

Roots reached out like fingernail scratches raking across the path. Some of the roots felt spongy with decay, and the green-black smell of wet leaves and soil was everywhere. I tried to walk around the worst patches of mud. I had brought a small backpack with my camera, water, sunscreen, bug spray, the contest list, and some snacks, but I didn't think to bring extra clothes. It'd be embarrassing to slip and end up covered in goo.

A few stripes of sunlight stretched across the path, and I glanced quickly along the side of the trail for anything colorful to shoot. Chipmunk-sized holes disappeared into the darkness between the roots of a big pine tree, and scattered around the tree were mushrooms in different sizes and colors. Tiny white umbrellas, bumpy tan bouquets, and a few squat ivory ones like marshmallows grew in the moss. A few feet away, there was even a tan flat one that looked like a pancake with one bite gone. Most of the mushrooms were too ordinary and plain to be interesting. But a little banana-colored umbrella mushroom caught my eye. I removed some distracting bits of bark and arranged some dark wet leaves behind it to make the yellow pop against the darker background.

"That's pretty," Nate said when I showed him my shot on the screen.

It *was* pretty, but I could just hear Dad saying there was no surprise in my photo, nothing to make it *more* than what it was. "Yeah, but it's only a mushroom," I said, deleting it.

As I walked behind Nate, I wished something amazing would happen — like a moose would cross the path ahead of us. But even when you're in a likely place, sometimes nothing happens. The animal doesn't come. Or he sees you first.

"The leader on the trail gets all the spiderwebs!" Nate waved his arm in the air in front of him. "They feel weird across my neck every time I walk into them."

"Do you want me to —?" I let out a little gasp.

"What is it?" Nate asked.

Against the rough bark of the tree trunk, the toad was almost invisible, blending perfectly except for his eyes. "Look right here," I said, pointing. "If he hadn't jumped, I never would've seen him."

Nate stooped beside me. "Hey, Mr. Toad."

It wasn't a moose, but it was *something*. Holding my camera away from me, level with the toad, I moved it slowly sideways. "I want the contrast of green leaves behind him, not just tree trunk," I explained. "The toad's probably less scared of the camera moving than he'd be of my whole body moving around him."

Trying to hold everything steady, I got off several shots before a drop of sunlight fell on the toad's face. He blinked and hopped into the ferns.

I switched on my screen. Most of the photos were terrible. In one shot, I had missed the toad completely.

But in one photo, the toad stood out beautifully against the leaves. I showed it to Nate.

"Wow," he said. "He really blends in with the tree trunk."

I nodded. "But his eye doesn't blend, and that leads you right to him. This is one lucky shot."

"No one who sees it will think that. They won't know you took a bunch of shots to get that one. Is there a contest word you could use it for?"

I took out my page and scanned through the choices. "It could be 'a closer look.' Or 'texture.' His skin is amazing, and the tree trunk has a different texture, but they work together well."

"'Texture' is a harder word," Nate said. "You can look closer at anything."

"You're right. Okay, this is 'texture.'"

As we walked, I couldn't help turning the camera on a few times and looking at the toad again. I thought it was a great shot, but what would Dad say?

The higher we climbed, the cooler the air became, but the faster I heated up. My T-shirt stuck to my skin, and I longed to take off my backpack so my shoulders could have a break from being pulled backward.

Three miles hadn't seemed too long in the trail parking lot, but it felt like forever as the trail grew steeper. Every time I'd see a steep section ahead, I'd get excited to reach the top, only to find another steep section beyond it.

Thank goodness Grandma Lilah hadn't come. We'd left the mud behind, but she never could've climbed over all these big rocks.

"Am I going too fast? Do you want to stop?" Nate asked.

"Sorry. I'm not used to this."

"That's okay." He sat on a big rock. "I'm glad to take a break. I don't understand people who hike like it's a race. What are they, excited to go back home?"

Sitting next to him, I was glad to let my breath catch up with the rest of me. Straight ahead was a screen of bare tree trunks, their only leaves high overhead, shivering in a breeze too far away for me to feel.

From off in the woods I heard a snap. *A moose?* I looked hard into the trees, but how could a moose even *fit* in between all those trees? It was probably a squirrel. In the quiet, everything sounds bigger. "I can't believe you and Grandma Lilah hiked up here."

"We did it every year for a while, but the last time we did it, she stepped between some rocks and fell. She didn't break anything, but she got scraped up, and Dad said that was enough."

"That's too bad," I said. "I could tell last night that she loved this hike."

Nate nodded. "I hate telling her no about anything, but it's harder for her to do lots of stuff she used to do. After my grandpa died, she moved in with us, but she still came to the cottage every summer by herself. This year, Mom was worried she might fall and no one would know. So Mom said we'd come, too, to make sure she's okay. We're doing all her favorite things. Loon Patrol and ice cream and cook-outs and watching old movies."

"That sounds great."

"Yeah, but I don't know if my parents will even *try* bringing her next year. So it's kind of sad, too. I start having fun, but then I remember this might be her last summer here. It's like I'm missing things that aren't even gone yet."

I sighed. "It's too bad you can't make everything exactly the way you want and then freeze it to stay that way."

Nate nodded.

"It's one of the things I love about photography," I said. "It's always 'now' in the picture. Even if everything else changes."

"If I could freeze time, I'd pick the last summer Grandma Lilah made it all the way up and down Cherry Mountain without falling and could go on Loon Patrol by herself." Nate paused. "Except then I'd be eight years old forever, and this summer has already had some good parts to it."

I glanced at him, wondering if meeting me was a good part. But he was digging in the pine needles at his feet with a little stick. "So maybe I'd freeze a day this summer when Grandma Lilah was doing well — even if she couldn't climb a mountain or get into a kayak."

"Can we freeze a day this summer that hasn't happened yet?" I asked.

"Sure. Why not?"

"Then I'd freeze a day this summer when Dad is home and Grandma Lilah is happy. With no thunderstorms, because Ansel doesn't like those."

Nate looked up from his stick. "We'll freeze a sunny day."

"With a breeze so there are no mosquitoes." *And Megan is somewhere else for the day. Like Antarctica.*

"Sounds perfect," Nate said. "Are you ready to hike again? We don't have far left to go."

As we continued upward, I thought about how adults sometimes complain that kids only think about ourselves, but it's not true. We care a lot about other people, but most times, we don't have the power to change things for them.

At the top of yet another steep climb, the trail widened and I could see patches of blue sky between the trees ahead, all the way to the ground.

"Almost there!" Nate said over his shoulder.

As the trail spread outward, I saw farthest-away first.

The sky.

Some white clouds.

The lightest blue mountains.

As I neared the summit, rows of closer mountains appeared, a darker blue. Blue upon blue upon blue, above a carpet of trees.

I imagined myself with a hang glider, speeding down the trail and jumping right off the ledges and out into all that air.

And from somewhere deep inside me, I found the extra push I needed to run the rest of the way.

Journey

From the top of Cherry Mountain, there are mountains in all directions, rippling like a rolling sea, wave upon wave. Wide open and windy, the summit cooled me off so fast it didn't seem possible that I'd been hot and sweaty only minutes before. I made my way carefully around the ledges and between the shrubs and small trees, looking for views to photograph.

But no matter where I stood, I could only fit a fragment of the mountains in the frame. And when I checked my shots, none of my photos compared with the real thing. They just couldn't show the hugeness I felt. The frame was too small.

Above the trees, everything seemed so close and touchable, like I could step from mountain to mountain and sit the tiny houses in the valley on the tip of my finger.

"That's Mount Washington," Nate said, pointing to the tallest peak, with its weather towers spiking up like tiny knife blades. "That summit's probably full of visitors and climbers on such a good day."

We waved to them, even though they couldn't see us.

Up here, everything looked wilder than it did from below: the forests, the bald patches of cliffs, the curving rivers, and the odd-shaped puddles of lakes. My knees felt shaky. It was weird to be in real wilderness. No guardrails, nothing to keep you safe. *You* had to do it.

"Don't get too close to the edge, or you might — ahhh!" Nate jumped off the ledge.

I gasped, but then I saw him standing on another step of ledge a bit below the first, looking pleased with himself. "Not funny!" I said.

He looked really happy for fooling me, though. As he was climbing back up, his phone chimed.

"It's Megan," he said. I watched his fingers typing back a response.

"What does she want?" I asked, trying to sound totally normal.

"She asked if I wanted to come over. I told her I'm on top of Cherry Mountain."

As he typed, I wondered if he was telling her that he was hiking with me. And if that would give Megan one more reason to dislike me. But Nate had come over to my house that morning, not the other way around. So really, if Megan was mad at someone, it should be *him*.

His phone chimed again, and I didn't even want to watch him reading his message.

"So are you and Megan good friends?" I asked.

"We've known each other since we were little. Usually I only see her for two weeks in the summer, though."

That sounded like regular friends, in-a-group friends, not *best* friends. But maybe Megan thought that since Nate was here all summer this year, they'd do all kinds of things together. Maybe she had thought they'd be best friends, even if Nate didn't think that. I opened my backpack and started taking out the snacks I'd brought so I wouldn't have to watch him answering her.

"Food! That's great. I'm starving." Nate put his phone in his pocket.

"Don't get too excited, okay? We haven't done much grocery shopping yet. So all I could find were some graham crackers and peanut butter and stuff to sprinkle on top." I pulled out unsalted cashews, a box of raisins, a little bag of granola, Christmas-colored sprinkles, shredded coconut, candy Red Hots, and dried cranberries. "Sorry. All we had was weird back-of-the-cupboard stuff that moved with us."

Nate reached for the crackers. "We can make graham cracker sandwiches. Like s'mores, only *not*!"

"We can call them 'No Mores'!" As I loaded up my peanut-butter graham cracker with raisins and coconut and sprinkles, a chipmunk darted from between the rocks. He rose on his hind legs a few feet from us — like a tiny striped prairie dog. "How does a chipmunk live up here? It must be cold in the winter."

"Chipmunks hibernate," Nate said. "So they miss the worst part of the winter."

"I wish I could do that," I said, tossing the chipmunk a chunk of my graham cracker sandwich. "I'd like to wake up and have skipped over the whole school year."

The chipmunk ran over and smelled the cracker, then used his tiny paws to pack it into his cheek.

"Me, too," Nate said. "The other kids think I'll have it easy because Dad'll be one of my teachers, but I won't. He'll be harder on me than anyone else."

"I have to be 'the new kid' — again." I sighed.

"I have an idea. Give me your camera." When I handed it to him, Nate sat next to me and held the camera to face us. "Hold up your 'No More'!"

I held up my cracker as Nate took a photo of us together.

"There!" he said, handing back my camera. "You said a photo would let you freeze time, right? So when you look at this photo, it'll be now again."

I turned on my screen. In the photo we were grinning like good friends. "Thanks."

"These 'No Mores' aren't bad," Nate said, making himself another. "This time I'll try the Red Hots."

I smiled. "Don't give any of those to the chipmunk. He might explode!"

We ate the whole package of graham crackers, except for a few bits I threw to the chipmunk. Then it was time for our secret plan. "Let me see the photo of Grandma Lilah and you."

Nate opened his backpack and took out the framed photo, wrapped in a navy T-shirt. "You won't wreck it, right?"

"Of course not," I said. "But I need it out of the frame. The glass will reflect too much."

Out of the frame, the photograph looked flimsy. I held it tight as it fluttered in the breeze. In the old photo, Grandma Lilah and Nate were sitting a bit off-center in a space between two big granite rocks. A small tree was at the left edge of the photo, with only blue mountains stretching across the background. "We have to find the exact place you were sitting," I said. "Let's look for these big rocks with a small tree next to them."

"The tree's probably bigger now," Nate said.

In the picture, Grandma Lilah was wearing a white baseball cap. There was a logo of some kind on it, but I couldn't read the words. She wore a yellow nylon coat and khaki shorts, her muscular legs disappearing into knitted socks and hiking boots. But it was her smile that my eye went to — bright and full of happiness. And beside her was Nate, small and giggling, in the circle of her arm.

"You had really short hair," I said. "And I love the Spider-Man T-shirt."

"I was five," he replied flatly.

"You look cute," I said. "It's a good photo. Did someone take it or did Grandma Lilah use a timer?"

"She had a timer, and we kept messing up when it would go off. She'd set up the camera and we'd rush over and sit down and then wait and wait. Just when one of us would give up, it'd go off. This was the only good photo. I wish she'd saved the others, because they were funny." He smiled, but his eyes looked sad.

"I wish I had taken more photos of the regular things from the places we've lived. They didn't seem important enough to shoot, but I miss them the most. You think you won't forget them, but you do."

Nate nodded. "When I take photos, I use my phone, but then I almost never look at them again."

"I've taken a few photos with my phone so far, but I can control things better with my camera. I can set the aperture and shutter speed. That lets me do special things like motion blur."

"Maybe I'd look at my photos more if they were as good as yours," Nate said.

Talking about photography made me wonder what Dad was doing. I hoped he was thinking about me.

Nate and I walked all over the summit, looking between the photo and the view around us. "I think this is the right direction," he said, stepping carefully over the ledges. "Grandma Lilah wouldn't have taken me anywhere too dangerous. Wait! Let me see the photo again. These might be the big rocks!"

Sure enough, they were the same two rocks. The little tree was taller now, but not a lot. The wind had kept it small. I held the photo out in the air in front of me. "If I line up the mountains in the photo and then include some of today's view around the edges in my shot, it'll look like·the old photo continues into the new one. It'll be like we brought her with us."

"But won't your hand be in the photo?"

"Yeah, but that's okay," I said. "Though maybe it would be better with *your* hand? Since you're in the old photo."

It was a great idea, but much harder than it seemed. To make it work, Nate had to stand completely still holding the photo in front of him in his left hand, but lean his head far to the right so I could shoot over his shoulder.

I reached around to move Nate's arm a little bit at a time until it all lined up with my eyes, and then I checked through the lens. The camera wouldn't be forgiving, and every time Nate wiggled or the wind shook the photo, we had to realign it all. Before long, I was practically hugging Nate from behind. I bit back a giggle.

"My arm is killing me," Nate said.

"Just a few more, okay?" It took lots of tries until I had one where the mountains lined up almost exactly from the new photo to the old one. And in the center Grandma Lilah and Nate looked so happy.

"Whew!" Nate said when I told him he could put his arm down.

"I can make a print," I said, showing it to him. "And we can give it to her."

"It's a cool photo, but —"

A sudden puff of wind took the old paper photo out of his fingers. It all happened so fast that I only had time to gasp. The photo landed on a bush on the edge of a ridge. "Be careful," I said as Nate raced down the rocks to get it.

"Let's go home," he said, snatching it off the bush.

My head hurt from that close call. What if the wind had been just a little stronger? The photo could've vanished forever in a second.

"I'm sorry." Trying to make it fun again, I joked, "But when we give Grandma Lilah the new photo we can tell her she had an adventure and nearly blew off the mountain in the wind."

"I wish she could've come with us, but I know she can't," Nate said. "I did have an idea about Loon Patrol, though, and how maybe she could do *that* for real."

"What was your idea?"

"She can't climb into a boat or a kayak anymore, but I've seen motorized rafts on other lakes."

"An inflatable raft?" I asked.

"No, these are regular wooden swimming rafts. Just like the ones people anchor out in the lake or attach at the end of their docks. They're usually square and have a ladder and maybe a diving board. But *these* rafts have a motor on one end. So you can just pull up the anchor and use the motor to drive it around the lake. If we had something like that, we could park it up against our dock and Grandma Lilah could just walk from the dock onto the raft. We could even put a chair on it for her. I mentioned it to Mom, but she said those rafts cost too much."

As Nate returned the old photo to its frame, I was amazed at how much he'd already thought this out.

I'd only been doing the contest for something fun to do with Nate and maybe to show off to Dad when he got home. But I already had some photos I was proud of: the loon on the nest, the kayak with Nate's cottage in the background, and the toad on the tree trunk. Would five hundred dollars buy a raft?

I wasn't sure if my photos would be the best. But if I did win and didn't use the prize money for myself, Dad might be more okay with me winning. He likes making a difference with his photos. How could he complain if I was trying to make a difference with mine?

As I considered it, I walked around the summit taking some photos. If I was really going to enter, I had to make the most of every chance now.

A tiny flower growing bravely in a crack in the rocks ("Hope").

The trail disappearing back into the dark woods ("Journey").

Nate from behind, taking a last look at the mountains around us ("On Its Own"). As he started down the trail, I took one more photo, trying to capture the dizzying drop-off, the heart-bursting vastness of it all ("Beyond Reach"). But I just couldn't make the photo compare with the real thing.

The person looking at this photo would just see what was there. They wouldn't know what was missing, but I'd know.

I took out my phone and texted Dad.

When you're shooting, do you ever find there's a scene that no matter what you do, the photo just isn't as good as the real thing?

Nate was already out of sight on the trail when my phone chimed with Dad's answer.

Every day. Sometimes you just have to live it, instead of shoot it.

Putting the camera down, I took a deep, cold breath, pulling it all inside me — the trees, the mountains, the sky — and held it as long as I could.

Then I gave up and turned for home.

Sticky

When Dad's away on a trip, not only do I get less of him, I get less of Mom, too. Mom and I have more chores to do, because someone has to do all the things Dad usually does at home.

So I love the special things Mom and I do when he's gone.

"I'll get the ice cream out of the freezer so it'll soften up a bit. And the grocery store had fresh strawberries," Mom said, taking boxes and cartons out of the refrigerator.

After washing and cutting some strawberries, I peeled the bananas and cut them into spears. "Did you get maraschino cherries, too?"

"Of course. What would banana splits be without cherries?" she asked. "We'll put those in a bowl. But let's be sure to leave some cherry juice in the jar, in case there are leftovers."

"Leftovers?" I joked. "Ha! Cherries are my favorite part!"

Picking three bowls from the cupboard and two spoons from the drawer, I said, "I'm going with sixty percent vanilla and forty percent chocolate ice cream in my bowl. But first, Ansel gets a little scoop of vanilla."

I didn't even get his ice cream to the floor before Ansel had his nose in the bowl. As he licked, his dog tags jingled against the side.

"I thought I'd put some shredded coconut on mine," Mom said, looking in the cupboard. "But I can't find it."

"Oh, sorry. I took it hiking with me," I said. "Nate and I made graham cracker sandwiches, and coconut was one of the toppings. I fed the leftovers to a chipmunk."

"You gave a chipmunk shredded coconut?"

"I told Nate not to give him any of the Red Hots, though. I didn't want the poor chipmunk to blow up."

She smiled. "Sounds like you had fun."

"I wish Nate and his family lived here year-round," I said, dipping a spoon into the hot fudge and drizzling it over my ice cream.

"You'll make more friends," Mom said. "You always do."

I nodded. It takes a while to sort out which kids really want to be long-term friends and which kids are just bored with their old friends, though. Sometimes kids want to be my best friend at first, because it's cool to be friends with the new kid. But that wears off, and when it does, that kid and all her old friends turn on you. I didn't want to explain that to Mom, though.

"Nate and I made Grandma Lilah a present," I said, to change the subject. "She can't get to the top of Cherry Mountain anymore, so I asked Nate to bring an old photo of the two of them together on the mountaintop. I took a new photo of him holding the old photo at the same exact spot. So it'll be like she came with us."

"What a thoughtful idea," Mom said. "Nate seems like a nice kid. I'm glad he lives next door."

"Me, too." Holding down the top of the whipped-cream can, I swirled and squirted a mountain. As I dropped several cherries on top, I thought about the contest. Maybe I could make this look "sticky"? I dipped my spoon into the edge of my whipped cream and dribbled some trails over the side of my bowl. I took a quick photo as Mom lifted her banana split toward me.

"To our new home!" she said, and we clinked our bowls together.

Everything began melting into smooshy deliciousness. We stopped talking, focused on eating. The tart strawberries made a nice change from the sugary sweet cherries. Halfway through, I added a new whipped-cream mountain.

"Want another cherry?" Mom asked.

"Of course."

Mom's cell phone rang. "Hello?" she said, answering it. Her face brightened. "Hi! How's everything in Arizona?"

Maybe Dad had tried to phone me first? I checked my phone to make sure the battery wasn't dead. Nope.

Waiting for my turn, I swirled my spoon through my melting ice cream. At my feet, Ansel had vanilla all over his nose and face. His tongue moved as far as it could reach in all directions, licking his face to get every drop.

Finally, Mom said, "Okay, here's Lucy!"

I grabbed her phone.

"Hello, sweetie!" It's always a relief to hear Dad's voice sounding so close. "I climbed a mountain," I told him. "I texted you from the top. And I've been kayaking."

"Wow!" Dad said. "See? Didn't I tell you you'd love New Hampshire? Did you go with Mom?"

"No, I went with Nate."

"A boy?"

"It's not like *that*," I huffed, though maybe it'd be okay if it was a *little* like that. "And there was a thunderstorm the night you left. Ansel, Mom, and I hid under my bed."

"That would've made an awesome photo!" Dad said.

I paused. Maybe I should've tried to shoot that moment under the bed? Ansel had been so scared that it hadn't even occurred to me.

"Just a minute! I'm coming!" Dad yelled to someone else. "Sorry, sweetie. I have to —"

"Are you getting some incredible photos?" I asked quickly. Even when he's busy, photography is a subject he'll talk on and on about.

"I have one that's a real *moment*," Dad said. "I can always shoot some good photos, but those real moments are as rare as almost never. But every now and then, something truly amazing happens at the very second you're ready for it."

"What's the photo of?" I asked.

"A snake springing after a baby rabbit. It's intense and beautiful. I didn't even know how great that shot was, because it all happened so fast."

"A snake? Aren't you supposed to be photographing some rare bug?"

"I got some solid shots of the bug," Dad said. "But developers want to build houses on this land, and not many people want to live in a house with snakes all around. So they want to get rid of them. But these snakes are almost as endangered as the bugs, and this photo would make an amazing cover for the magazine."

"Was the rabbit okay?"

"The rabbit? Oh. No, but the snake has to eat. There are a lot more rabbits than snakes. He worked hard for it."

I didn't want to argue with Dad, especially since I had barely gotten to talk to him at all. But I didn't want to see that photo, because I like rabbits a lot. "I took some photos of the loons for you. Remember how you asked me to do that?"

"Great! I have to go now, sweetie. Everyone's in the van. They're waiting for me. Give Ansel a pat for me, okay?"

"Okay," I said. "Love you."

"Love you, too."

My ice cream had turned soupy. How could I want to talk to him so much and then feel worse when I finally did?

"He said it's hot in Arizona," Mom said. "But not humid."

"He's taking pictures of snakes," I told her. "In one photo, a snake is killing a rabbit."

Mom made a face. "Let's hope he doesn't want to put that one on the living room wall."

I moved my spoon through my ice cream, thinking of the photos I'd shot. They were all good or okay. But if I really wanted to win the money to help Nate get that raft, I'd have to do better.

I'd need some "moments."

9

Wonder

Most things get easier the more you do them. With each box I unpacked with Mom, there weren't as many decisions to make. Now we just put things where they belonged: silverware here, pots there, mugs in the cupboard closest to the sink, books on the bookshelves, mail on the table next to the door.

And every time I went on Loon Patrol, I felt surer about kayaking: how hard or gentle to pull on my paddle to avoid hitting the other kayaks, and the angle I needed to hold the paddle at to keep water from dripping on my legs.

I wondered if by going on Loon Patrol so often, I was adding more reasons for Megan not to like me. But I wasn't going to stay home just because of her.

"At breakfast, Grandma Lilah put the teakettle on and then went into the living room and forgot all about it. The whistle made her jump off the couch. She thought it was a loon yodeling outside!" Emily laughed, dipping her paddle in the water next to mine.

"Some days the loons feel like they're part of our family," Nate said.

"Yeah, but if they were *really* part of our family, Mom would yell at them for waking us up so early," Emily said.

I reached down to lay my hand flat on the water. It felt like I was holding the whole lake under my palm. Mirrored in the water around my fingers, the blue sky was full of frail, stretched-long clouds. I pulled my camera out of my life vest and shot a photo of my hand, surrounded by water-clouds.

I wondered what my fingers looked like to the fish underwater. Then I heard a splash at the shore. *A snapping turtle?* At the edge of the bank, trees leaned out over the lake; their roots, as big as my arm, snaked between the rocks, creating lots of hiding places. Whatever had splashed had ducked out of sight.

Stay away from our baby loon! "Can the loon chick swim as soon as it's hatched? Or do the parents need to teach it?" I asked.

"It can swim right away," Nate said. "But the parents teach it to dive and fish."

"It's funny to watch them feed it," Emily said. "The adults catch minnows and give them to the baby, beak-to-beak."

"I hope we get to see that," I said.

"They'll stay near the nest until the second egg hatches or until they give up on it," Nate said. "After that, they'll leave the nest for the summer and swim all over the lake."

"The cutest thing is when they teach the babies to make the different loon calls," Emily said. "Sometimes we'll hear tremolos or yodels and think the loons are in danger. But when we look through the binoculars, there's no danger. Grandma Lilah says they're teaching their baby what the different calls mean and how to make them."

"We call it loonsong lessons," Nate said.

I grinned. "I love that."

Sitting forward in my kayak, I pulled my life vest backward to let some air circulate. Crossing the lake, there was no shade, and my back was getting sweaty under there.

An ant walked across the nose of my kayak. He must've climbed on when the kayak was back on the sand and now found himself at sea with me, hitching a ride. I pointed him out to Emily. "When we get back, he can go home and tell his ant friends about his big adventure on the high seas. I hope he —"

My voice was drowned out by a speedboat zipping across the lake, pulling a kid on an inner tube. The waves from their wake rushed toward me, rocking me sideways.

"I wish the motorboats would be more careful," Nate said. "The loons get scared when they come too close."

"And it doesn't just scare them," Emily said. "If the parents spend too much time watching out for boats, they don't bring up enough food, and the chick starves."

How awful. It was bad enough that other animals wanted to eat our chick, but at least that was understandable. "Maybe we could make some signs?" I suggested. "Because boaters might be more careful if they knew that."

"That's a great idea!" Emily said. "We could put a sign at the boat landing so people who are launching their boats will know to be careful."

"We could hang another at the marina. They rent

boats to people who are visiting," Nate said. "Let's walk down to the store when we get back and buy some supplies."

"I can take photos of the loons with the chick to put on the posters," I said. "So people will know what to look out for."

Now I had two ways my photos might help! Maybe they could help Grandma Lilah see the loons, and maybe they could help the loons be safe. As we entered the cove near the loons' nest, water streamed along the sides of my kayak, and my paddle kept picking up the long strings of the lily pads. A swarm of spidery bugs swirled along on the surface, like they were skating in a wild hockey game.

A dragonfly landed on my shorts, a stick of neon purple. I was used to seeing the electric-blue ones, but this was the first purple one I'd seen.

I worked my camera slowly out of my life vest and managed two close-ups of the dragonfly before he suddenly zipped off into the air, hurrying to who-knows-where.

"Look!" Emily said. "Both of the adult loons are in the water. And there's the chick!"

The two adults were swimming close to the nest, the baby riding on one parent's back. The nest looked lonely without a bird on it, one egg left behind.

"Maybe the second egg is a dud," Nate said.

"At least they have one." But my joy for that fuzzy, busy little chick had a center of sadness inside. *Is this how it ends? Just half-good?*

"It might still hatch," Emily said. "Though I wish one of the adults would get back on the nest. The egg will cook in the sun."

One of the adult loons hopped awkwardly onto the nest and turned the egg over with his bill. He settled himself carefully down on the egg.

"Oh, good!" Nate said. "They're still taking care of it."

The chick struggled to follow the adult up onto the nest. It wasn't a high jump for the adults, but the chick was so small, he had to try several times before he finally wiggled up the side.

Emily laughed. "He's too cute!"

A sooty puffball with a white belly, he walked like a floppy puppet. It'd be hard for people to ignore something as adorable as that baby loon. I zoomed in and took photo after photo as he climbed around the nest and over his parent's back, and then dropped back into the water. He scrambled up onto the swimming parent's back and cruised by the nest.

"It's hard to get a good shot of him, because he doesn't stop!" I clicked and clicked, hoping my photos wouldn't be blurry. Maybe one would even turn out to be a "moment" and surprise me.

As we paddled home, I looked backward at the nest and the adult loon patiently waiting there. "Maybe we shouldn't put a photo of the loon on the nest on our posters?" I said. "Because people might go looking for the nest. And that might disturb the loons."

"I think it's okay," Emily said. "Because if that egg doesn't hatch in the next day or so, it probably won't. And then they'll leave the nest area until next year. It'll take at least a couple days to make the posters and hang them up around town."

"Okay," I said. "Before we go to the store, I just have to go home and tell my mom."

But when we got back from kayaking, Grandma Lilah was on the dock with Nate's little cousins, Morgan and Mason. The twins had been making mud pies on the dock. Piles of sand, decorated with sticks and rocks, plastic buckets and shovels, were everywhere.

"We can go swimming now!" Mason yelled.

"You could've gone," Grandma Lilah said. "I'm right here to watch you."

"Mama said we had to wait for Nate and Emily and the other girl," Mason said, jumping off the side of the dock.

I blushed at "the other girl," but he hadn't said it mean.

"Sorry," Nate said to me. "I thought we could go, but I guess we have to help watch the little kids. Do you want to go swimming?"

I opened my mouth to tell him I had to go home to change, but then I realized Nate was going in with his clothes on.

Why not? I was really hot, so I took off my life vest and left my camera and my phone on the dock next to Grandma Lilah.

When I stepped into the water, the bottom was so sandy, it gave way under my feet, heels first, almost to my ankles. But as I walked out farther, the bottom turned gooey and gucky with rocks and old slippery leaves and pine needles and I-don't-even-want-to-know-what. I pushed off quickly into a breaststroke so I wouldn't have to touch.

"It's freezing!" I said, my teeth chattering.

"Nate, pretend you're a shark!" Mason said. "Say 'I'm gonna get you!'"

"Me, too!" Morgan said. "But don't *really* grab me, okay?"

"Okay. I'm gonna get you!" Nate dove under, but I let myself float. The water cooled my skin and lapped against my ears. It's funny how cold lake water always feels when you first get in and how warm it becomes as you get used to it. I felt so relaxed, like I could fall asleep right there, except I could hear Emily talking to someone. "And Lucy took some photos of it!" I heard her say. "We're going to make posters to tell the speedboaters to stay away a safe distance."

I rolled over in the water to see Megan pick up my camera from the dock. "I want to see the chick, too. How does this work?"

"I'll do it!" I didn't want her touching my camera. As I swam toward the dock, she said, "That's okay. I have it on now. Cool! I want to help with the posters, too."

When I got out, my hair was wet and clumpy and my shorts stuck to my legs. I pulled my T-shirt out in front so it wouldn't be clingy and embarrassing.

I took my camera from her and picked up my phone. "I'm heading home to change," I said to Emily. I didn't want to leave, but I couldn't hang around in wet clothes.

"Bye, Lucy," Emily said. "I'll let you know when we go to town. It may not be today, though. Morgan and Mason can swim forever."

"We're gonna swim until there's *ice* on the lake!" Mason yelled.

On the walk home, I texted Dad.

The loons have a baby! SOOO CUTE!

Then I clicked on my camera's screen to look at my loon photos, but the first photo that came up was the purple dragonfly. Where were my photos of the baby loon? I clicked and clicked, but the dragonfly was the last photo on my card. My photos of the chick were gone.

Every last one.

10

Now and Then

"I hope the Baileys like potato salad," Mom said the next night as we crossed our driveway toward their cottage.

"That spoonful we tested tasted good to me." I've always wanted to live someplace where the neighbors invited us to cookouts. So when Mrs. Bailey came over to ask us, I stood behind her and nodded my head fast at Mom. I'd been wondering when would be a good time to give Grandma Lilah the photo I'd taken on Cherry Mountain, and a cookout seemed perfect. Nate had carefully returned the old photo to its spot on their cottage wall, and I'd made a print of the new photo and put it in a frame. Wrapped up, it looked like a real present.

"I hope Grandma Lilah doesn't mind that the only wrapping paper I could find was birthday paper," I said to Mom.

"It doesn't say 'Happy Birthday' on it. Confetti and balloons could be for any celebration," she said as Mr. Bailey waved to us. "I'll bring my potato salad over there to the table. Do you want me to take your present?"

"No," I said. "I want Nate to give it to her."

Grandma Lilah and Nate's parents were talking to some adults I didn't know. Neighbors, probably? Aunt Pat was scolding Morgan and Mason for running with sticks in their hands.

I looked around for Nate, and I tried to keep smiling when I spotted Megan sitting with him and Emily and some younger kids I didn't recognize on their cottage porch.

Megan greeted me with, "I didn't know you were coming."

"I didn't know *you* were coming, either," I said evenly.

"I always come," Megan said. "Nate, remember last summer when we played croquet with the kids who rented the Poules' cottage? You hit the ball so hard, it made a big dent in the side of their porch."

Nate nodded. "Mrs. Poule was pretty mad."

"*We* should do that again. And remember the old guy who rented the Macleods' cottage a couple summers ago? Mr. Tidal Wave?"

Nate grinned. "He used to cannonball off his dock," he explained to me. "And he was a really big guy, so the splash was ginormous!"

I smiled, though I was pretty sure Megan was bringing up these old stories to make me feel left out.

She glanced at me. "Who's the present for?"

"It's for Grandma Lilah." I knew the smartest, safest thing would be to leave it at that, but I couldn't help getting back at her a little. "It's a photo from when Nate and I climbed Cherry Mountain."

"Lucy is awesome at taking pictures," Nate said. "She's doing a photography contest and I'm helping her. It's a scavenger hunt."

"It's just for fun, really," I said, not wanting Megan to see how important it was to me.

"But if you win, you get money," Nate said. "So it's not *just* for fun, right?"

"Hey, Lucy, how'd your photos of the baby loon turn out?" Emily asked. "I still want to make those posters."

"My photos *didn't* turn out," I said, not looking at Megan. "Every one I took of the chick got erased somehow, except the very first one of him on the nest when he'd just hatched."

"Oh no!" Emily said. "How'd that happen?"

"I don't know, because it was only *those* photos." I slid my gaze over to Megan. Her face was red, but she didn't say anything. I was pretty sure she'd done it on purpose. Because when someone wrecks something by accident, they say sorry.

"Don't worry," Nate said. "We can do Loon Patrol tomorrow and take some more photos. It's Dad's turn to go, but I bet he'd be glad to give it up."

"And maybe there will be *two* chicks now," I said. "That would make for even *better* photos than the ones that got deleted."

"That would be great!" Nate said. "We'll go tomorrow. Then we can go to town and get poster board and stuff."

Megan shot me a look as friendly as poison ivy.

But I just nodded. "The sooner we get the posters up, the better."

After supper and s'mores and my first-ever game of flashlight tag, which was really fun even though I was "it" a lot because Megan tagged me every chance she could, Nate whispered excitedly to me, "Let's give Grandma Lilah the photo now."

"You do it," I said, all tingly with eagerness. "It's from both of us."

The adults were talking, but Nate walked right into the middle of their group and laid the present in Grandma Lilah's lap. "Lucy and I have a present for you," he said. "We made it — well, sort of. You'll see!"

Grandma Lilah ran her hand over the balloons and confetti wrapping paper. "How lovely! I didn't know it was my birthday," she said, sliding her finger under the flap.

"Sorry," I said. "That's the only wrapping paper I could find."

"It's a rectangle," Morgan said, running up beside her. "Maybe it's a book!"

"Or a game!" Mason said.

Grandma Lilah pulled the framed photo out of the paper.

"It's us!" Nate said. "Lucy and I climbed Cherry Mountain and we brought you with us. See?"

"Isn't that wonderful!" Mr. Bailey said. "How did you manage this?"

Nate grinned. "I held the old photo and Lucy took the new photo standing behind me. It was hard to line it all up. We had to try and try, a whole bunch of times. My arm was dying."

"We climb Cherry Mountain every year," Grandma Lilah said. "We should do that."

"You went up there with Nate and Lucy this year," Mrs. Bailey said. "There you are right at the top of the mountain, Mom!"

I thought Grandma Lilah would be happy and touched that we did this. But she looked confused. "We could go tomorrow. What day is it today?"

"At the lake, it doesn't matter, does it?" Mrs. Bailey said kindly. "It's summer, let's leave it at that."

"What's the weather report?" Grandma Lilah asked. "Is it a good day for climbing?"

"It's supposed to rain tomorrow," Nate said. "We can't hike in the rain."

"Anyone for another s'more?" Mrs. Bailey asked, too brightly. "We have plenty of marshmallows. Mom, can I make you one?"

"We'll climb Cherry Mountain tomorrow," Grandma Lilah said firmly.

"It's going to rain, Mom," Mrs. Bailey said, sounding tired. "There's no view in the rain."

"We need the rain," Mr. Bailey added. "It'll be good for the gardens and the grass."

"It's best to get an early start," Grandma Lilah said. "Wear some good shoes."

"Lucy, I think we should go. It's getting late," Mom said.

"Must you go already?" Mrs. Bailey asked, but she was watching Grandma Lilah, not us.

"We've had such a nice time, everyone," Mom said. "Thank you for inviting us."

Nate followed me to the edge of the driveway. "I'm sorry. Grandma Lilah gets a little mixed up when she's tired," he said. "She got up with the loons this morning and she didn't take a nap."

"That's okay," I said, even though I felt like crying.

"I'll show her the photo again tomorrow morning," he added. "She'll like it then."

I nodded. "Sure. Don't worry about it. It's okay."

But all the way home, I thought about how my photo had ruined the cookout.

11

Secret

On a gray, calm day, the lake becomes a mirror, reflecting other things: trees, cloudy sky, the ghostly outline of the mountains. It matched how I felt. Upside down and not really myself.

When Mom and I came home from the cookout, she told me she thought something was wrong with Grandma Lilah. Not just the ordinary kind of getting older and forgetting a few things, but maybe something bigger.

"I think she might have dementia," Mom said.

"What's that?" I asked.

"It's difficult to explain," Mom said, "but it's a brain disability that happens to some people when they're older. When I was your age, my aunt had dementia and we used to visit her sometimes. She had a hard time doing certain things and understanding and remembering — even things she'd done her whole life. No one really knows why it happens."

"You never told me about your aunt," I said.

Mom shrugged. "As a child, I didn't like visiting her. It was always sort of confusing and sad. She didn't even seem like the same person anymore."

"Did she get better?" I asked.

Mom shook her head. "My mother stopped bringing me when my aunt didn't know who we were." She put her arm around me. "Lucy, I just don't want you to take it personally, what happened. The photo was a lovely idea, and if Grandma Lilah were completely herself, I'm sure she would've loved it."

Nate had told me they were doing all Grandma Lilah's favorite things this summer, and it had seemed nice when he said it. But now, I could see that maybe it was more than that. Maybe they were doing those things because she was still "her" enough to enjoy them.

I wanted to apologize to Nate, but I didn't know how. So the next morning I texted him.

Will we go on LP if it rains?

It seemed like a safe topic to start with, and I was relieved when my phone chimed almost immediately.

Yes, unless it thunders. But E has 2 watch M&M.

At ten o'clock, I met him on their beach. I had thought maybe it'd be easier to apologize to Nate without Emily. But I still didn't know what to say.

"Is Grandma Lilah coming down to see us off?" It felt weird not to have her on the dock with us as we left.

"No," he said.

I couldn't look at him, so I watched the zipper of my life vest as I pulled it up. "I'm sorry about last night. I thought she'd like the photo."

"Me, too," he said, picking up his paddle. "But she talked so much about climbing Cherry Mountain last night that we had to hide both photos."

I winced, getting into my kayak.

"Mom and Dad got into an argument about whether it was getting too hard to take care of her here," Nate continued. "Dad thought it was and Mom thought it wasn't."

If Grandma Lilah had to go home, Nate would go, too.

And I hated the thought that the last thing they did here this summer would be a sad thing. Last times and first times shouldn't matter more than all the middle times, but somehow, they do.

I pushed off with my paddle from the shallow water and stroked hard to catch up to him. "Remember how if I won the contest, I'd get some money? Well, I've been thinking. If I won, maybe we could use the money to buy one of those rafts you talked about, the ones with the motor on them. Then we could take Grandma Lilah out to see the loons."

Nate dipped his paddle slowly. "Really? You'd do that?"

"Do you think it would make her happy?"

He nodded. "She'd *love* that."

"We'd just have to buy the raft and get it here," I said. "But I might not win."

"You have a good chance, Lucy," he said, smiling. "I think your photos are great."

Normally, it would've made me feel warm inside to hear him say that, but as we paddled our kayaks toward the nest, the secret I'd been keeping weighed on me. I wasn't sure how to tell him, so finally, I just let it all out in a rush: "I do have one problem, though. My dad is the judge of the contest."

"What?" Nate stopped paddling. "Your dad is the judge?"

"I read the rules really carefully, and there's no *rule* against me entering," I said. "So I don't see how it could be cheating."

"Why didn't you tell me? All this time we've been working on the contest," Nate said. "I thought we were good friends."

I couldn't help liking that he said we were good friends. I had thought so, too, but it felt nice to hear him say it. "We *are* good friends. I should've told you, but it was fun taking the contest photos with you even if I didn't enter. But now I want Grandma Lilah to be able to do Loon Patrol herself, in case — well, I just want her to go."

I felt like I was babbling. "The rules said the photos had to be originals, and they probably expect kids to use their real names, but it doesn't say we have to. So I've been thinking. Maybe I could make up a name. If I use my real one, I think Dad would worry it wasn't fair or be extra hard on me because he'd have to show everyone else that he wasn't playing favorites."

From the corner of my eye, I watched the nose of Nate's kayak come back into view.

"One bad part of having a dad who's famous is sometimes it feels like I can't have photography as my thing, just because he got there first." I peeked to see if Nate was mad.

But he nodded. "I get tired of everyone lumping my dad and me together at school. Adults say, 'Oh, you're Mr. Bailey's son!' And kids say things like, 'Don't tell Nate, because he might tell his dad.' And then I have to decide if it's worse to be in trouble with the other kids or with Dad." Nate pulled harder on his paddle. "But if you won, the prize money would probably come as a check. You wouldn't be able to cash it if it wasn't your real name."

I felt all the air let go from my lungs. "Oh. I didn't think of that."

On the far side of the lake, a thick layer of mist rose like smoke from the water. Nate dug in his paddle to stop. "I can't tell if the loons are on the nest or not," he said. "But do you see that great blue heron over near the reeds? You can just make out his shape in the mist. That would make a cool photo."

I didn't feel like shooting, but there was a wonderful moodiness to the mist and the heron stood so still and tall. It was a relief to do something I knew how to do. Normally I'd zoom in for a bird, but the heron looked so mysterious in that stripe of fog that I left the scene wide.

"You could use my name and address for the contest," Nate said.

I opened my mouth to say no. Using the real name of someone else seemed more wrong than using a pretend name for me. But somehow the word got stuck in my throat. Nate and I had been working *together* on the contest. I was taking the photos, but he was giving me good ideas and helping me choose. We were a team, even if the contest only allowed for one name. It wouldn't be cheating to simply choose his name instead of mine, would it?

I felt a drop of rain on my arm. Within seconds, the lake around me had hundreds of circles, all of different sizes, in motion on the surface. The heron took to the air, and I was glad I'd taken that shot while I had the chance.

"We should go back," Nate said. "In case it starts to thunder."

I tucked my camera way down into my life vest so it wouldn't get wet. We paddled steadily, racing each other for the dock as the rain came on. As I moved my paddle from side to side, I weighed the pluses and minuses of using Nate's name. If we won we could use the money to help Grandma Lilah see the loons — and that was a big plus. *Dip and pull.* But on the minus side, if my photos won, I'd have to pretend the photos were Nate's, and he was *in* one of the photos I was planning to use.

Though it would be great to know for sure that my photos had won or lost on their own. *Dip and pull.* But I couldn't shake off the nagging feeling that it wasn't "right."

I wasn't trying to make any other kids lose — just trying to give my photos a fair chance to win. *Dip and pull.* But Dad might get mad if and when he found out.

He always said it's about the photos, not the photographer. This would give him a chance to prove it. *Dip and pull.* But we might not even win.

Though we'd never know if we didn't enter.

"Nate, how about this?" I suggested. "What if we use your name until Dad picks the winners. The portfolios will be mailed to my house, so I'll be there when he chooses. I can ask to see the winners before he sends off the results to the magazine. If it's us, I can tell him then. If he thinks it's unfair that his own kid won, I could pull our portfolio."

"And if he lets us win?"

"We'll use the money to get Grandma Lilah out to see the loons," I said.

Nate's phone chimed. He didn't even look to see who it was. "If there's any money left over, maybe we can build Ansel his super-swanky kid-and-dog house?" he said.

I grinned. "It's a deal!"

As we got closer to the dock, I could see a splash of bright yellow ahead. Grandma Lilah was standing with an umbrella, waiting for us. "How are the loons?" she called.

"Just fine," Nate called back. Even though we hadn't seen them.

12

Holding On

Every time someone in Nate's family did Loon Patrol, they answered Grandma Lilah's question of "How are the loons?" with "Fine" or "Good" or "They were teaching the baby to dive today."

But the secret answer was that no one had seen them. A few times we'd heard them call and my heart leapt, but we couldn't be sure if it was our loons we were hearing, or visitor loons just passing through.

The next time it was my turn for Loon Patrol I could barely wait for ten o'clock. But first, Mom needed help unpacking the last boxes of Dad's books and equipment. Then Ansel wanted to play, and I hadn't been spending much time with him, so I threw his stuffed sheep toy and he brought it back, again and again, until finally he got tired. Then at ten o'clock, just as I was leaving, Dad called Mom on her phone. I couldn't pass up the chance to talk to him, even though I had to wait for her to talk first and the connection wasn't good. I kept asking "What?" and glancing at the clock, hoping Nate and Emily would wait for me.

"No one's seen the loon family for a few days," I told Dad. "We're worried."

"What?" he asked.

"We haven't seen the loons!"

"I'm sorry, I can't hear you. I'll try calling again later, okay? I love you."

"I love you, too," I said. "Next time, try my phone!" But he didn't answer, so I don't know if he heard me or if he'd already hung up.

By the time I arrived at the Baileys', Nate and Emily had already left. Grandma Lilah motioned to the empty white wicker rocking chair beside her on the porch. "Come wait with me. Nate thought you weren't coming."

She looked so hopeful that I couldn't say no. "I didn't mean to be so late. I had to do a bunch of stuff this morning, and then my dad called right when I was leaving." I was shocked that my voice broke as I spoke.

"What's the matter, dear?"

"I miss my dad. That's all. I didn't even really get to talk to him because he couldn't hear me very well."

"It's hard when people leave you," she said. "And hard when you leave them, too."

I nodded. We were talking about sad things, but it made me feel a little better knowing I wasn't alone.

A hummingbird buzzed up to the hanging baskets on the porch, his tiny wings blurring with speed. From inside the cottage, I could hear Morgan and Mason making car sounds and Nate's dad explaining something to someone.

Maybe I could paddle out and catch Nate and Emily? But when I looked over at the beach, the pink kayak wasn't there. Of course the Baileys could do whatever they wanted with their kayaks, but the pink one felt partly mine now. "Did someone go kayaking with Nate and Emily?"

"Yes, I think so," Grandma Lilah said.

Megan? "Um, was it a kid?"

Grandma Lilah looked concerned, so I changed the subject to one I knew would please her. "I was hoping to get some photos of the baby loon. We're going to make posters so the boaters will be more careful."

"What a lovely idea," she said. "You can take *my* photo while we're waiting. Just like I'm a movie star!" Grandma Lilah rolled her left shoulder forward. Dipping her chin, she batted her eyelashes, pretending.

Where was Nate? I glanced to the lake, hoping to see him coming. But the water in front of the cottage was empty. When I looked back at Grandma Lilah I couldn't help giggling because she looked so funny, joking with me. "Okay. Hold that pose. Let me try an angle that's not straight-on," I said. "Are you Marilyn Monroe?" It was the only old movie star name I could think of.

"Doris Day!"

From somewhere on the lake, a tremolo reverberated. As Grandma Lilah looked toward the sound, I took the shot. "Oh, I hope that's our loons!" The words were barely out of my mouth before I remembered that she didn't even know they'd been missing.

"Can you see what's happening?" she asked. "The tremolo is a warning."

I looked toward the lake, but I didn't see that familiar dash of black body and head above the water.

"Emily said the parents give the chick loonsong lessons," I said to comfort her. "I bet they're just practicing."

She smiled. "Loonsong lessons."

I checked my screen to see the photo of Grandma Lilah. There was worry in her eyes as she stared at something beyond the frame. Anyone who saw the photo would wonder what she was looking at. It added a touch of mystery to the photo: something to think about beyond the image itself. It added a story.

"I've never watched the loons come in the spring and I've never seen them leave in the fall," Grandma Lilah said. "They're always here when I arrive and they leave after I go."

"They're like the summer people," I said, trying to make a joke.

"I might not come back here next year," she added quietly.

"I'm sure you will," I said.

She shook her head. "I'm not well. My family thinks I don't know, but I do. Next year everything here will happen without me. But *I* won't be the same without it."

I didn't know what to say. I glanced to the lake, hoping I'd see Nate coming, but the lake was still empty.

"Oh, dear. I'm rambling, aren't I?" she said, blushing. "I'll be better when I've had a rest. What were we doing?"

"Taking photos," I said.

"You must take my photo."

"Okay," I said, relieved to have something to do. "Let's try another pose. Could you put your hand on the arm of the rocking chair?" One of my contest phrases was "Holding On," and Grandma Lilah's hands were so wrinkled and old that they would make an interesting photo.

"Maybe it's the weather," she said, gripping the arm of the chair. "Soon I'll get back in the swing of things. Maybe tomorrow."

I nodded and took some photos of her hand. "It's been a bad day for me, too. It feels like the universe is being extra mean today. So let's *both* hope tomorrow is better."

"And not worse," Grandma Lilah said.

I picked up a teacup from the table near her. It still had a little tea in the bottom. Her rough, ridged hands would be a wonderful contrast with the glassy smoothness of the cup. "Maybe you can hold this cup now?"

"It's almost empty," she said.

"That's fine. It's only for the picture. When someone holds something, it shows a relationship. It can make for a more interesting picture." I smiled. I sounded just like Dad.

As I took the shot of her hands holding the cup, she said, "Let me get you some more tea."

"No, thank you." I hadn't had any tea at all, and Nate *still* wasn't coming, so I zoomed out to shoot her whole body in the rocking chair with the teacup in her hands. The rustic boards of the cottage behind her would make a good background. "Tell me about this cup," I said, hoping to get some emotion on her face. "Where did you get it?"

"It's not mine."

"No? Oh. Well, it doesn't matter. Do you like tea or coffee?"

Grandma Lilah's face clouded over with concern. "This is not my cup."

"Do you want a different one?" I asked quickly.

Grandma Lilah's eyebrows climbed with alarm. "It's not mine!"

My finger pressed the shot. "You're right. I'm sorry." I took the cup from her. "It's my cup."

"Hey, Lucy! There you are!" Emily called. "We waited for you as long as we could."

Thank you, universe! I turned around, so glad to see Emily and Nate coming up the beach that I didn't even mind that Megan was with them.

"We saw the loons!" Nate said.

"I even took some photos with my camera!" Megan said.

Nate's smile faded as he got to the porch. He looked from Grandma Lilah to me. "Is everything okay?"

"Fine!" But my voice sounded higher than usual. Grandma Lilah still looked upset. And it was my fault.

"Did you see the chick?" I asked.

"Yes, but we had a surprise!" Emily said. "There isn't just one chick! There are *two*!"

"They're so cute!" Megan said. "One baby was trying to dive, but he could only dip his head in the water. Then they both got onto their parents' backs. I got photos of it all for the posters."

"Let me see!" Grandma Lilah said, the fear melting from her face.

Part of me wanted all Megan's photos to be dark and blurry and awful and unusable, but they weren't. In fact, one photo of an adult with the two chicks on his back was really good.

"Two chicks!" Grandma Lilah said. "Two chicks! Write that down, Nate!"

"I will," he promised. "Lucy, we're going to town now so we can get poster board."

"I'm going," Megan said.

"Me, too!" Grandma Lilah said. She looked okay now, but my insides still felt all twisted for upsetting her. I didn't even know how it had all gone so wrong so fast.

"You want to go, Grandma Lilah?" Nate asked, hesitantly. "All right. We won't walk, then. Let me see who can drive us."

I wished we could do this later. But the deadline for the contest was coming up. There might be some photos in town.

And Megan was going. One thing I know about being in a three-way friendship is that you'd better not let the other two spend too much time without you, or it turns into a two-way friendship, minus you.

"Okay," I said. "Let me run home and get some money."

13

Collection

From the parking lot of Barton's Grocery, I could see the entire length of Main Street in my new town, from the white, tall-steepled Methodist church at the north end all the way down to the Catholic church at the south end. Between the churches stood a row of little stores and businesses. Good Value Hardware, Frank's Gas and Auto Body, Mitty's Snowmobile Rentals (CLOSED FOR THE SEASON), Raven's Ice Cream Shoppe (OPEN FOR THE SEASON), a white fire-and-rescue building with big red vehicle doors, Pizza

Junction, a small post office, and an old house with a sign that read THE LAKEVIEW GIFT SHOP (ONE-OF-A-KIND GIFTS AND TREASURES).

On the short ride to town, Megan had chatted with Emily in the backseat of the van about the posters we were planning to make to help the loons.

Those posters had been *my* idea, but I couldn't talk to anyone. Grandma Lilah looked fine now, but I was bruised by what had happened. I couldn't stop rerunning our conversation in my head.

Nate leaned my way to whisper, "Is there a good contest word we can find in a grocery store?"

The contest seemed so far away, but it was a relief to think about something I knew how to do. Point and shoot. And if you did it wrong, you just deleted that shot and tried again.

I thought about some of the words I still needed to shoot. "Left Behind." "Lost." "Collection."

"Maybe 'collection'?" I whispered back.

He smiled. "How about a collection of fruit?"

Could fruit be a collection? I supposed so, but when I had stepped out of the van, there were lots of people in the grocery store parking lot, pushing carts and talking and hurrying in and out of the store. It'd be hard to take a photo in the store without being in other people's way.

"I'll catch up," I said as Mrs. Bailey helped Grandma Lilah out of the van. "I'd like to go in the gift shop for a minute." The gift shop probably had better choices for "Collection," and it didn't feel like anything would be right until I had a minute by myself to think about what happened.

"What a good idea!" Grandma Lilah said. "Let's all go!"

I sighed, but there was nothing I could do.

White with blue shutters, The Lakeview Gift Shop had no view of the lake, just of Pizza Junction across the street.

Bordering a walkway to the gift shop door were wooden boxes of daisies, black-eyed Susans, lavender, and herbs. A sign next to the entrance read COME IN! SORRY, NO STROLLERS. LEAVE BACKPACKS AT THE FRONT DESK. WE WELCOME WELL-BEHAVED CHILDREN HELD BY THE HAND.

Friendly, but don't push it.

Stepping into the gift shop, I was greeted with the overwhelming smell of flowery soaps and balsam pillows. On the long shelves were rows and rows of candy, jelly and jam, mugs, stuffed animals, and magnets. This place had collections of collections!

"Welcome!" said the woman behind the counter. "Nice to see you all back this summer!"

"Mrs. Stackpole, this is Lucy," Mrs. Bailey said. "Her parents bought the Alexanders' house."

"Lovely to meet you, Lucy," she said. "Are you here just for the summer or year-round?"

I forced a smile. "Year-round." Picking up a jar of strawberry jam, I held it up to the window light. The red jam was vibrant lit from behind, and a line of different colored jams on the windowsill with the sun shining through might be pretty. But lit from the back, the labels on the jars would just look like black rectangles in a photo, and that would ruin it.

"All the jam is New Hampshire–made!" Mrs. Stackpole called.

I put the jar back. Wandering through the kids' area with picture books, plastic boats, and beach floats to inflate, I considered the shelves of stuffed animals: moose, foxes, chipmunks, black bears, and birds that made their calls when you pushed a button on their back.

"I wonder if Ansel would like one of these?" I asked, looking through the birds. I pushed the button on the blue jay and it screeched. "Yikes! That would drive Mom crazy," I said, putting it back.

"Oh, look, Grandma Lilah," Nate said. "They have a loon." He pushed the button and a loon's wail sounded in the store. I was glad the toy company had picked the loon's "checking in with each other" call and not one of the danger calls.

Grandma Lilah smiled. "I'm here! Where are you?"

Nate pushed the button to answer. "I'm here."

"Are you done, Mom?" Mrs. Bailey asked. "We're heading over to the grocery store. You kids come over when you're ready."

"I'm ready now. Come on, Megan," Emily said.

I held back as Megan walked toward the door with Emily, Nate's parents, and Grandma Lilah. "I'll be right there," I said. "I want to buy something here."

"I'll wait for Lucy," Nate said.

Megan shot him a glance, and I wondered if she'd stay, too. But Nate wasn't looking at her and didn't see the letdown in her eyes.

I know what it feels like when you want to matter to someone and they don't notice. But I was still mad at Megan for deleting my photos and trying to take over my idea of the posters.

Only when I heard the front door of the gift shop close did I dare peek over. It was just Nate, Mrs. Stackpole, and me now. *Whew.* As my shoulders dropped, I tried to let go of my hard morning. "I thought this would be a better place to find a 'collection' photo," I said to Nate.

It was all such a jumble that my photo would look cluttered — not really like a collection. I walked through THE CHRISTMAS CORNER with its ornaments, wooden deer, Santas, and cards. In the back of the shop were lamps, blankets with camp designs, and signs that looked old, but really weren't.

I glanced at wind chimes, bird feeders, tiny baskets woven with pine needles, and the displays of books and calendars and tourist brochures near the register. Dad's book *New England Places and People* was facing out on the top shelf. It was an older book, all the photos taken before I was born. But seeing a book I recognized and his name on the cover made me miss him so much I could barely look at anything else.

"What about candles?" Nate asked. "There are lots of different sizes and colors."

I tore my gaze away from the books. I had to hurry up and pick something, because I didn't know how long it'd take Nate's family at the grocery store. I was ready to settle for the candles when I noticed a jar of rock candy. Each wooden stick ended in a finger-long burst of colored sugar crystals wrapped in clear plastic — a jar full of long, bumpy lollipops. Bright pink, blue, green, yellow, white, purple, red, and orange.

Nate grinned when I showed them to him.

None of the candies were exactly alike. I took a light-blue one from the jar. The crystals closest to the middle were darker, packed tight on the stick, but the ones on the outer edges had just a hint of blue. I held it in front of the window and watched the sun shining through, reflecting off all those sharp-cornered little squares.

I picked as many different colors as I could find. As Mrs. Stackpole was ringing them up on the register, I said, "Wait a sec. I want one more thing."

Nate looked surprised when I returned to the cash register with the toy loon.

"Ansel needs a new toy for New Hampshire." I plopped it down on the counter with the candy.

We were ready to leave, but the light coming through the window was great. "Maybe we can shoot the photo here?" I asked Nate.

"Okay," he said.

How best to show a collection? Lined up? In a pattern of colors? I wanted the light to reflect on and through all those little squares.

"Mrs. Stackpole, would it be okay if I borrowed a cup so I can stand these sticks up on the windowsill? I'll put everything back when I'm done," I promised. "I want to take a photo of my candy, and the light is so pretty right now."

She hesitated, so I added, "Did you know that you sell a book of photos by my dad? It's on the top shelf: *New England Places and People*."

"Really?" Mrs. Stackpole looked quickly at her bookshelves. "Do you think he might come for a signing? Or at least stop in and sign the copies we have in stock?"

"He's in Arizona right now taking pictures for a magazine," I said. "But when he gets home, I know he'd be *delighted*."

I took her pleased smile as an "okay" to choose a small ceramic juice glass from the pottery shelves and move the boxes of maple sugar candies away from the windowsill. I handed my rock candy to Nate. "Can you unwrap these? Light will bounce off the plastic. Your brain knows to ignore the wrappers, but a camera only shows what is."

As Nate unwrapped, I stuffed the bottom of the glass with leftover plastic so the rock candy would stand higher and I could fan out the sticks to allow light to pass between the different colors.

When we'd arranged them, I shot photos from different angles. But when I checked the screen, I was disappointed. "The cup makes it look like it's a bouquet of candy, not so much a collection," I said. "And with the cup in the shot, it's about the cup, too." I tried zooming in, cutting the cup out of the frame.

Much better. Now all that showed was brilliant-colored, light-filled candy, and in the background, a pleasant gray blur from the window light.

As soon as I had several shots that could work for "Collection," we put our rock candy in the bag with the toy loon and returned everything else to the way it was. "Ansel will like that his new loon toy smells like candy," I said.

Walking with Nate to the grocery store, I opened my bag and took out a stick of pink rock candy. "Want one?"

Nate chose orange. "Hey, you didn't tell me your dad had written a whole book." He bit off the top of his candy, and crystals scattered down his shirt.

"He's done lots of books." I let my candy sit in my mouth, my tongue dissolving the bumps of sugar. Rock candy was pretty, but it was hard to eat. "I wonder if Emily found the poster board?" I said as we threw our sticks into the trash can just outside Barton's automatic doors. "It's probably —"

"Where's the door?" Grandma Lilah was screaming from somewhere inside. "Help me!"

Nate ran into the store and I followed, searching the aisles, until we finally found her in the cereal aisle. A broken bottle of salad dressing was on the floor at her feet, and beside her, Mr. and Mrs. Bailey's faces were red.

"Just take her outside," Mrs. Bailey said. "I'll pay for this and the other groceries and walk home."

"You can't walk home with all the groceries!" Mr. Bailey said.

"Well, come back for me, then!" she snapped. "Please just take her home!"

Nate took Grandma Lilah's arm. "Come on, Grandma Lilah. The door is over here."

Strangers kept talking around us like they didn't notice, but I knew they did. A lady's eyes met mine over the top of a display of juice and a family stared at us from the end of the aisle. A boy with glasses and floppy hair, wearing a red grocery store uniform shirt, looked down our aisle and said, "Don't worry. I'll get the mop and clean that up."

"Grandma Lilah, come this way. You'll see the door," I said comfortingly.

She just stood there, not moving, even when Nate pushed the back of her arm, encouraging her to take a step.

I pulled the camera out of my pocket and rushed far enough down the aisle to shoot a photo of the automatic doors ahead with the EXIT sign over them.

"Look, Grandma Lilah." I hurried back to show her on my screen. "See? The doors are right over there. Follow me, and you'll see them, too." I started walking, hoping I'd hear the soft sound of footsteps.

I didn't realize I'd been holding my breath until I heard her coming and felt the air rush out of me.

All around us, people were having a regular grocery store experience:

"Let's look in the dairy aisle."

"Are you sure that's the right size?"

"Here it is!"

An older lady with short gray hair, wearing her purse strapped across her body, was talking on her cell phone in front of me. She looked at us curiously but didn't step aside. I wanted to yell at her, "Just move!"

I must've looked scary, because she immediately did.

"See you folks," the cashier called as I led Nate and Grandma Lilah out the exit. "Have a nice day!"

Outside, the van seemed a million miles away, even though it was only across the parking lot. Megan hurried to get ahead of us, holding the stack of poster board in front of her like a big white shield for us to walk behind.

For once, I was glad she was there. People in the parking lot looked at her, not at us.

As Nate coaxed Grandma Lilah into her seat of the van, I let my head fall backward to look at sky. It was a relief to see something faraway and endless after being so tightly focused on each breath and step with Grandma Lilah.

On the drive home, Nate's parents argued in the front seats. "Why didn't you bring her in through the main door?" Mrs. Bailey asked. "That's the door I always use."

"How would I know it'd make a difference?" Mr. Bailey asked. "I didn't *plan* to cause a scene."

"I caused a scene," Grandma Lilah said sadly beside me.

"No! I'm sorry," Mr. Bailey said quickly. "I didn't mean that."

"Don't worry." Mrs. Bailey turned around to face Grandma Lilah. "It's fine, Mom. Accidents happen."

"I couldn't find how to get out," Grandma Lilah said. "I thought you all left."

"We were getting milk," Mr. Bailey said.

"Megan and I were buying poster board," Emily said.

"We thought you knew that," Megan added. "I'm sorry."

"We wouldn't go home without you, Mom," Mrs. Bailey said. "Why would you think that?"

"I don't know. Yes, of course," Grandma Lilah said. "That's right."

Sitting next to her, I wondered what I could say to comfort her. My dad would know the right words, but I had no idea.

After a pause, Mrs. Bailey said too brightly, "Lucy, how's your mom?"

"Um, she's good," I said. "She's working today."

"It was so nice to meet her at the cookout." Having moved the conversation back to a more normal place, Mrs. Bailey turned to face forward again. But she leaned her elbow against the car door and her head against her hand.

I glanced over my shoulder to Megan with Emily in the far back. Megan looked as uncomfortable as I felt to be in the middle of Nate's family's hard times.

"It's a bad day," Grandma Lilah said quietly beside me. "Someday I worry I might slip into one of these bad days and not come out."

"Mom, don't say that!" Mrs. Bailey said. "It doesn't do any good to think like that."

Grandma Lilah looked so defeated that I pulled the loon toy out of my bag. "Grandma Lilah, I bought you something."

On my other side, Nate whispered to me, "But that's for Ansel."

I shrugged one shoulder at him and pushed the button on the toy's back to play the loonsong.

Grandma Lilah didn't smile, but as I laid it in her lap, I heard her whisper, "I'm here."

That night, we didn't make posters. I sat on my bed with Ansel and downloaded my photos. I chose the best rock candy photo for "Collection." Then I scrolled through my photos of Grandma Lilah on her porch. I smiled at her pretending to be Doris Day. But in the last photo, Grandma Lilah was sitting up very straight, holding the teacup. That photo was all about her eyes. Full of panic, they seized me and wouldn't let me go. I could hear Dad in my mind gasping with me at what I had captured.

A true and terrible moment.

14

Design

It took every drop of willpower not to tell Dad about the incredible photo I had taken of Grandma Lilah on her porch. But I really wanted to use that photo in the contest, so the next day while I waited for Nate and Emily to come over to make the posters for the loons, I texted Dad about everything else.

Ansel says "Woof."

I hope the snakes do something amazing. But not with rabbits.

I saw a newt at the mailbox. He was orange! But when
I came back with my camera, he was gone. Grr!

Mom's making brownies. Nate and Emily are coming
over today.

Ansel barked like crazy at the knock on our front
door. "I'll get it!" I yelled to Mom as I put my phone
back in my pocket.

"The brownies are almost done," she said. "Do
you have everything else that you need?"

"I think so. Nate and Emily are bringing the supplies," I said.

As I crossed the living room, I could already see
through the window that there were three kids on
our porch. Nate and Emily and Megan.

"Hi," I said hesitantly as Megan stepped past me
into our living room. I'd been sure she'd stay home
when she discovered we were making the posters at
my house.

"Hi." She looked from one side of our living room
to the other, and I wondered if she was comparing
it to hers.

"Wow! What smells good?" Nate asked.

"Mom's making brownies," I said.

"Lucy, do you know that I've been coming to the lake my whole life, but today's the first time I've ever been inside your house?" Emily said. "The Alexanders were old, and I don't think they liked kids very much. So they never invited us in. It's nice in here!"

"Thanks," I said. "Everything creaks, but I'm getting used to it."

"Everything creaks at our cottage, too," Nate said. "And one year, we had bats! They had moved in over the winter while we were gone!"

"I remember that year!" Megan said. "Your dad was trying to catch them and Grandma Lilah was yelling, 'Don't hurt them!'"

They all laughed. I pretended I thought it was funny, too. But really, you probably had to be there.

"The table's not big enough for all of us," I said. "So I was thinking we could work on the floor. Go ahead and set up and I'll get us the brownies and some lemonade."

In the kitchen I let the forced smile drop off my face. "There's four of us," I said quietly to Mom. "Megan's here, too."

"That's nice," she said, and then paused. "Isn't it?"

I shook my head, taking the lemonade out of the refrigerator. "She wants to be Nate's only friend."

"In a month, all this will change," Mom said comfortingly. "Don't let it get you down."

She probably thought she was making things better by reminding me that Nate and Megan and their families would leave at the end of summer. But I only wanted little things to change, not big things. And Nate leaving until next summer was a really big thing.

When I came back to the living room with lemonade and cups, Ansel was walking over the word LOONS! on Nate's poster.

"Ansel, go lie down!" I said.

He did, right on Emily's poster. "He wants to help!" she said, rubbing his tummy. He rolled right onto his back for her.

Mom came in behind me with napkins and a plate with the brownies stacked so high that we could each have two or maybe even two and a half. "Ansel, come!" Mom said to get him off Emily's poster.

Ansel obeys anyone holding food.

I took a brownie off the top and passed the plate to Emily. "I made prints of each of my best loon photos in case anyone wants to use one on your poster." I showed them the copies: the adult loons swimming and the loon on the nest watching me, the baby under her wing. "This is the only photo I have with a baby." I glanced pointedly at Megan. "Did you bring *yours*?"

She looked away from me. "I realized this morning that I don't have a way to print them. We brought a laptop with us to our cottage, but not a printer."

I didn't want to help Megan. But I *did* want to help the loons, and showing the babies was important. "If you go get your camera, I'll print them. I'll even use photo paper so they'll look great."

"I'll be right back," she said.

While Megan was gone, I stared at the empty piece of poster board, wondering what to write. These posters would be hung up at the marina and the boat launch and other places where tourists would see them. How do you make people notice a poster, read it, and then care?

Watch Out for Loons! I wrote at the top, but I wrote "loons" in fat pillow letters so I could draw the checkerboard pattern of their wings inside each letter. With the rest of the space, I could probably fit three photos in a line down from the words. Maybe I could put one loon fact next to each photo? Underneath my heading, I glued my own photo of the female on the nest with her head down and the chick under her wing.

Don't bring your boat any closer to loons than 150 feet. Then I cut out a speech bubble and glued it so the baby under her wing could say, "BACK OFF!"

When Megan knocked on my door again, I had my poster well started. And both Nate and Emily had used the photo I took of the loon on the nest.

"Even though the loons are done with their nest now, it's a great photo," Nate said. "It reminds you that they're a family."

Megan handed me her camera's memory card. As she started her poster, I picked her best photos and printed a few sheets of copies. As each sheet came off Dad's printer, I brought it to Emily and Nate to cut apart into single photos. I hadn't seen both loon babies yet, and looking at Megan's photos, I wondered which one was the first chick. I'd never be able to tell them apart, especially from a distance. I decided to call them Baby One and Baby Two.

When I was done printing, I chose two of Megan's photos of the whole loon family to put on my poster. Next to one photo, I wrote: *If loons spend too much time watching out for boats, they can't bring up enough food for their chicks.* I cut out two more speech bubbles and made the babies say, "I'm HUNGRY!" and "Me, too!"

And beside the last photo of the loons, I wrote: *Whatever affects the loons affects everything else.* I cut out another speech bubble and had one of the chicks say, "Including YOU."

At the very bottom I wrote, *Please be careful. Sincerely, Lucy.* And then on impulse I added *of the Loons* to my name.

"I think Lucy has the best poster," Emily said. "It's strong, but it's also a bit funny so people will remember it. Lucy, why don't you put yours at the marina? Megan, yours can go at the boat launch. Nate's can go at the grocery store, and I'll ask Mrs. Stackpole if I can put mine at the gift shop. That should cover most places where tourists go. Right?"

"And not just the tourists," I said. "It'll remind the people who live here to be careful, too."

Winning the contest wouldn't matter if there were no loons for Grandma Lilah to see.

At the marina, I was nervous asking, but the man at the boat rental desk said I could hang my poster on the wall behind him. "Everyone who rents a boat will see it here. Are these loons from our lake?" he asked, pointing to the photos.

I nodded. "We have a family of four. Two adult loons and two babies."

"That's great! Visitors will love to know that," he said. "Loons are very popular."

"Please tell people they have to be *careful* of them. Okay?"

"Sure." While he hunted for some tape to hang up my poster, I looked out the big storefront windows at the rows of Jet Skis, kayaks, and speedboats hitched up to the docks.

"Do you rent motorized rafts?" I asked.

"Motorized rafts? No. I've seen those on other lakes, but that's something a cottage owner would *buy*. Not much call to rent those."

"Do you know how much it might cost to buy one? Would it be more than five hundred dollars?"

He nodded. "I'm sure it'd cost more than that for a new one."

"Oh. Okay." I tried not to let my disappointment show. "Well, if you had, um, let's say a grandmother who couldn't climb into a speedboat or a kayak, do you rent something that would work to take her out on the lake?"

"A pontoon boat would probably be a good choice," the man said. "My aunt uses a walker and I've taken her out on ours. Pontoon boats are good and stable and there isn't much climbing, just a step really. As long as someone is there to help her, I wouldn't think there would be any problem."

"Is it less than five hundred dollars to rent one?" I asked.

"About half that for a whole day."

"Thanks!" I smiled, though I felt like cheering. "That's really, really helpful."

Now all I had to do was win.

15

Three Feet

As the days passed and the deadline for the contest came closer, I stopped waiting for photo opportunities to appear and began to create them.

"How come Emily can show both her feet and I only get to show one?" Nate asked, taking off his sneakers.

"Mine are prettier," Emily said.

"Three Feet" was one of those phrases that can mean different things. Nate and I debated our ideas: a yardstick against a tree, three of Ansel's pawprints in the mud, or a shot from underneath the dock with three kids' feet dangling in the air between the bottom of the dock and the top of the water. The last one seemed like the best idea. But now that I was wading into the lake, cringing at the gooey bottom and imagining what *else* might be in the dark water under the dock, it felt cold and gross.

Though if Dad could survive billows of black flies and mosquitoes for hours, I could survive some icky under-the-dock dwellers for a few minutes.

Near the shore by the Baileys' dock, the sand was ridged by the waves. Standing there, I estimated how many steps I'd have to take in the mucky part before I was out deep enough to duck underneath the dock. I guessed about six big steps.

I wouldn't have chosen such a sunny day for this shot, but I didn't have time to wait for the weather to be perfect, and Megan had gone on a day trip with her parents, so she wouldn't be able to ruin anything or take it over. She had texted Nate when we were deciding what to shoot for "Three Feet" and invited him to go, but he stayed home to be the third foot.

He'd chosen me over Megan. So why didn't I feel happier? Because he had sighed when he texted her back. So at least part of him had wanted to go.

"Look!" he said. "The chicks are swimming with their parents."

Glad to have a reason to put off dunking under, I searched the waves until I saw the outline of the two adult loons and two little ones paddling hard to keep up. *There they were!*

The babies were diving, but it wasn't long before they popped to the surface again, like Ping-Pong balls. I knew they had to learn to dive and hunt on their own, but I couldn't help wishing they'd climb onto their parents' backs where it was safer. By themselves, other animals could take them: eagles and hawks from above, snapping turtles from below.

Dad says every animal needs to eat something. But these felt like our loons, and I would protect them if I could, just like I'd protect Ansel if anything tried to hurt him.

"Are you ready for your camera?" Nate asked.

"Almost." *Time to get this over with.* The water made me gasp with cold as I dropped onto my knees, wet to my shoulders. Then I pulled in a breath and went under the dock.

Underwater, I raised my hand into the air above my head so if there were a crossbeam above me, my hand would find it first. Touching only air, I let my head come up.

Nate's eye looked down through the dock slats above me. "How is it under there?" he asked.

I shivered. The sand felt slimy, and I hoped I wouldn't feel a crayfish walk over my toes or a fish swish against the back of my legs. "Cold and disgusting," I said, my voice echoing. "I'm ready for my camera now."

As soon as my camera appeared next to Nate's and Emily's feet, I took it carefully. "Nate, I need just one of your feet. But can you both turn to the left a little? I want to see more of the sides of your feet, not just the back."

The dark, rough underside of the dock was a nice frame for their feet. And it provided a good contrast with the sparkly waves ahead. Emily had a braided band tied around one of her ankles, which drew your eye and added a little bit of personality.

I didn't have enough room to move around under the dock and try many different shots, but I did the best I could. When I had a few I thought would work, I passed my camera out to Nate and eased my way from under the dock.

"Grandma Lilah will want us to write down that the babies were both swimming and diving by themselves today," Emily said. "I'll go get the clipboard."

As she left, one of the loons gave a throaty tremolo. "I don't see anything bothering them," Nate said. "Can you see anything with your zoom?"

I zoomed in as tight as my camera would allow and took some shots of the loon family together. "No, they look fine," I said. "I don't see anything that could be bothering them."

"Probably loonsong lessons," Nate said.

Climbing up onto the dock, I said, "We can show Grandma Lilah these photos of the babies swimming."

"Can I see the 'Three Feet' shots?" Nate asked.

I turned on my screen and handed him the camera.

He nodded, scrolling back through. "These are great! They're funny, because with just three feet, you wonder where the other foot is." He hit the scrolling button. "Oh. Thanks a lot for taking this photo of the EXIT sign at the grocery store that day. It was a big help."

I smiled. "You're welcome."

He scrolled again. "Oh, wow! The rock candy shots look great, too! These are awesome, Lucy." He scrolled again and his face changed. "What's this?"

It was the photo of Grandma Lilah with the teacup.

My smile slipped. "Oh. I took that one the day you went on Loon Patrol with Megan. Grandma Lilah and I were waiting for you to come back and she asked me to take her photo. She told me she was Doris Day. There are more if you scroll back. I thought we could use the photo of her hand on the rocking chair for 'holding on' and this one —"

"She looks awful." He hit the button to scroll, but his eyebrows stayed down.

"I was just making conversation," I said, hurt. "I thought if she talked about the teacup, she'd have an expression on her face. So I asked her where it came from and she said it wasn't hers. She got upset and I didn't know what to do. So I said the cup was mine. It only lasted a few seconds, though. Then you came back from Loon Patrol and told her there were two baby loons. That made her happy."

"It's a horrible picture of her," Nate said, shutting off my camera.

"It's not horrible." I tried to explain the way Dad would say it. "Her face has strong emotion and it draws you in. It makes you care about her."

I had looked carefully through the words of the contest, and one word stopped me. Grandma Lilah was losing things inside herself. She said it herself, that day.

"I think we should use it for 'lost,' " I said.

Nate didn't look at me as he gave me my camera. "There are a million photos you could shoot for 'lost.' It doesn't have to be that one. Besides, she's not even really lost. She's scared, and that's not the same thing at all."

"But don't you want to win?" I asked. "We can't take Grandma Lilah out to see the loons if we don't win."

"I'll pretend to be lost for you."

That night, I saved the best "Three Feet" shot and the best one of Nate in the little patch of woods near the lake pretending to be lost. But the photo of Nate looked fake, like an actor overdoing it.

When the picture of Grandma Lilah came up on my viewer, I pushed the button to edit.

DELETE? YES OR NO

It was a truthful photo, even if that truth wasn't beautiful. At first, it hadn't mattered about winning. But now I wanted to. If it were just a regular photo, I could let it go because Nate wanted me to. But this photo was amazing. There was a powerful story in her eyes, and Dad would see that immediately.

When Nate looked at it, he saw his grandmother, the person he loved. I couldn't make him understand that sometimes a photo was more than that. It had a regular truth you could see with your eyes, and a second one that you felt. This photo would make the person looking at it experience something important. And that made it special.

It made it art.

But when two things matter, how do you know which one matters more? What Nate saw when he looked at it? Or what other people would feel?

DELETE? YES OR NO

I shut the camera off so I didn't have to choose.

Later, I lay in bed with my hand resting on Ansel's chest, rising and falling in sleep. It was so quiet I could hear his breath and the waves down on the beach in rhythm with each other.

I couldn't sleep, couldn't turn my mind off. Why did my best photo come with the hardest choices? It didn't seem fair. And whose photo was it? Did it belong to Grandma Lilah because she was in it? Or did it belong to me because I had taken it?

There wouldn't even *be* a photo if I hadn't taken it. But it wouldn't be powerful without her. I finally fell asleep listening to the loons' nighttime wailing. And they woke me again before sunrise.

I'm here. Where are you?

I stared at my dark ceiling, waiting for the answer. Waiting.

But when the answering call finally came, it startled even Ansel awake. The male was yodeling.

Maybe the dad was giving the babies loonsong lessons? I held my breath, expecting him to stop.

But tremolos and more yodels came instead, one after the other so fast that it didn't sound like the loons could even be taking a breath between them. This wasn't practice. They jolted me out of bed and to my open window. I strained to see something. Somewhere on the dark lake, the loons were in trouble.

16

Lost

Getting dressed in the dark, I didn't even know what I could do to help the loons. I just knew all those frantic tremolos and yodels coming through my open bedroom window meant they were in trouble.

Nate and Grandma Lilah were already on the beach when I got there. Nate was dressed, but barefoot. Grandma Lilah was in her nightgown, looking through the binoculars. "What's happening to the loons?" she snapped. "Where are they?"

"Shh. You'll wake everyone," Nate said.

A tremolo sounded. Grandma Lilah started for the lake, like she was planning to walk right out over the water.

"Wait!" Nate ran after her. "Where are you going?"

"I'll go!" I said quickly. "Don't worry, Grandma Lilah. I'll scare away whatever is bothering them."

"Come back inside, Grandma Lilah. Please? Lucy will check on the loons. She'll make sure they're okay," I heard Nate say as I raced to get a paddle and life vest from under their porch.

Come on, come on, come on! It seemed to take forever to get my life vest zipped and the kayak in the water. But even as Nate pushed me off in the direction of the tremolos, I still had no plan, no idea what I would do.

I paddled as fast as I could. The sun was rising as I crossed the lake. It sounded like the loons' calls were coming from somewhere on the other side. Only when I reached the middle did I see one of the adult loons. His wings were outstretched, his feet moving fast, like he was doing a furious, jerky dance. Upright, he was almost running on the water; his bottom feathers only skimmed the surface. He looked like he was trying to take off and fly, only to fall clumsily, headfirst, into the water.

Was he hurt? The loon popped up a second later and yodeled. *That must be the male.* Where were the female and the chicks?

Scanning the water, my eyes caught a movement high in the trees. A flash of white head and dark wings.

I gasped as the eagle leapt off the branch and plummeted toward the water. The female loon and the babies dove as the eagle reached out for them. He skimmed the water, his talons almost touching the waves.

Missed! The loons surfaced: Mom, Baby One, and Baby Two. As the eagle circled for another pass, I paddled harder. If I could scare him, maybe he'd leave.

He came in for another swipe, his talons spread wide like hands. "Go away!" I yelled, waving my paddle in the air to distract him as the loons dove.

Missed again! The eagle circled around, but this time, he flew back to the tree and landed on a branch. *Yes!* If I could keep him away long enough, maybe he'd get too tired and have to give up. The mother loon and babies popped up again. I wished the little ones could stay underwater longer.

Please don't hurt them, I begged the eagle. *Please give up.*

But he didn't. Each time he swooped, I yelled, and each time he came up empty, my heart beat harder.

My arms ached, but I kept waving and paddling, trying to catch up to the loons. He wouldn't come near the babies with me right there. *Would he?*

But the loons kept swimming away from me. "Wait!" I swung my paddle again in the air to scare the eagle. "I'm trying to help you!" I yelled.

The eagle soared in again, so low over the water that he could brush the waves with his feet. The loons dove as the eagle's talons stretched out, snatching at the surface with a splash.

He had something.

Please let it be a fish! But my eyes filled with tears, because I knew it was a little loon clutched in his talons.

Drop him! I pleaded as the eagle flew off low over the waves. The loon baby would already be hurt, but I could scoop him up and get Mom to drive me to an animal hospital somewhere. He could still be okay. *Just drop him!* But the eagle rose into the trees, holding tight. On a branch, he dipped his beak to his talons.

And I couldn't watch.

The mother loon swam fast on the water, Baby One behind.

I don't know how long I floated there, feeling the sideways rock of the kayak. The lake was quiet again, just the ordinary morning sounds of birds and insects and the leaves shaken by the morning breeze.

When I finally dared to peek back at the trees, the eagle was gone.

I'd done everything I could, but I still felt like I had let everyone down. Maybe I had taken too long getting dressed, and I should've just gone out there in my pajamas. Or maybe I could've paddled harder. Or shouted louder. I clenched my teeth, hating that eagle. He had just swooped in and snatched our loon baby away from all of us.

Nature isn't always right. One life matters. Nate and his family wanted this to be a special summer, full of things Grandma Lilah loved. How could I tell her? Cupping water into my hand, I tried to wash my face so she wouldn't know I'd been crying.

They were waiting on the dock. "Are the babies all right?" Grandma Lilah called.

Behind her, Nate looked exhausted. He shook his head "don't" at me. When we hiked Cherry Mountain I didn't understand why he didn't want to tell Grandma Lilah the truth, but I understood now. There was nothing anyone could do. So why hurt her?

"Are the babies all right?" she asked again.

"Yes," I lied. "They're fine."

17

Left Behind

An eagle killed one of our loon babies, I texted to Nate when I got back home so he'd know the truth.

Oh no! We won't tell GL. OK?

OK, I agreed.

But I had to talk to someone before I exploded into pieces. Mom had been sympathetic, but she didn't understand. And Dad was worse. When I texted him, An eagle killed one of our loon babies. I saw it happen, he had texted back, I'm sorry you had to see that. But remember that the eagle needs to feed his babies, too.

That's MEAN! I texted back. I was so mad that Dad took the eagle's side that I deleted his message and turned off my phone so I wouldn't have to hear him apologize.

Nate and Emily were the only people who would understand. So even though I felt raw and knew it'd hurt even more to see the loons with only one baby, I walked next door at ten o'clock for Loon Patrol.

"We'll tell you what the loons are doing when we get back," Nate said, handing the clipboard to Grandma Lilah.

"They'll be teaching the babies to fish soon," Grandma Lilah said. "I wish I could go with you and watch them."

"We'll tell you everything we see," Emily promised.

But as soon as we were well away from shore, I couldn't hold it in anymore. "At some point we have to tell the Loon Preservation Committee." I moved my pink kayak slowly behind Nate and Emily. "They're trying to protect the loons. They can't do that if they don't know the whole truth."

"They don't need to know today," Nate said.

Emily nodded. "It's not like there's anything they can do. When the summer's over, we'll write what happened on the last survey form after Grandma Lilah has signed it. She doesn't have to see it."

Could we really hide it from her for the whole rest of the summer?

Near the middle of the lake, an adult loon swam with Baby One behind. Did they remember there used to be two babies? Do wild animals even have memories like that? Or do they only know "now," and move on without looking back?

The adult loon dipped his head low to look underneath the waves, then curled his neck, rolling forward to dive. Maybe it's kinder not to remember, because you don't have to grieve.

Please hurry. Don't leave the baby alone. I knew the adult had to fish to keep them both alive and deaths happen in nature all the time and no one notices. But this one mattered to *me*.

I looked around at the treetops moving in the breeze. "I wish the eagle had picked a fish," I said. "The lake has those to spare."

"Me, too," Emily said. "But the fish probably don't think that."

She was right. There was no way to win. I wanted the eagle to eat. Just not something I loved.

"I've been thinking if Grandma Lilah looks through the binoculars and only sees one baby, we can say the other was under the parent's wing," Nate said. "Or he's swimming on the other side of the adult. You don't always see both babies together, even when there are two. She seemed okay with —"

Nate's text chime sounded so out of place on the lake. I watched his kayak swaying as he worked his phone out of his pocket.

"We aren't doing anything this afternoon, are we?" Nate asked, reading his screen.

The way he said, "we aren't" hurt my feelings. After what happened that morning, I wanted someone to spend the day with. I wanted a friend. Why wouldn't he know that?

"I *did* want to finish the contest today," I said.

Nate didn't immediately say, "Okay," so I added softly, "But I can do that myself."

"What words do you want to do next?" Emily asked. "Maybe I can help?"

" 'Left behind,' " I said pointedly.

"That shouldn't be too hard," Emily said. "Maybe you could take a photo of someone walking away?"

Or driving away with Megan?

"But a person walking away might just look like someone going on a trip," Nate said. "Maybe if Emily had dropped something on the road behind her? Like a dollar? That would be the 'left behind' part."

"That would look too staged," Emily said.

"I could paddle away," Nate suggested. "And Lucy could shoot you from behind watching me go. *You* could be the 'left behind' part."

I didn't have time to think of something better. When I had started the contest, it had seemed like I had lots of time and a million possibilities. But now I had to get my entry in the mail — even if the last photos were only "good enough" and not everything I wanted them to be.

"I wish I could take a photo of Ansel looking out the window, because he has the saddest 'left behind' face ever," I said. "But Dad would recognize him immediately."

So I settled for a couple of shots from behind of Nate paddling away and Emily looking after him. But as I was shooting, my eye caught something else. Grandma Lilah was standing on the dock, waiting for us to come back. From this distance she looked tiny.

I zoomed in to cut our house out of the frame, but not close enough that you could read any expression on Grandma Lilah's face. Nate couldn't object to *that*.

I took a photo of her waiting for us, alone.

Left behind.

18

Your Name

I waited in my room for Megan's car to come and take Nate to I-don't-know-where. Maybe it was some place cool that he'd never been before and that's why he said yes so fast.

Or maybe he felt guilty that he'd said no to Megan before and wanted to make up for that.

Or maybe our friendship was about me being the new kid next door, and that newness had worn off and he was going back to the friend he had before me.

Lying on my stomach on my bed, I heard a car door slam and the sound of tires on a dirt driveway.

Part of me wanted to watch him leave, but the rest of me didn't move. I didn't even know why it bothered me so much that he was doing something with Megan, except maybe because I liked him as a best friend. And maybe he liked me as a for-now friend.

Beside me, Ansel poked me with his paw. "No," I said.

I wondered what Nate and Megan were talking about. It felt like the rest of the world was going on around me and without me. All I wanted to do was feel sorry for myself, but Ansel pushed me with his nose. The front end of him bowed down and the back end pointed up, tail wagging, wanting to play.

"Not now!" I snapped, and his tail stopped wagging.

"I'm sorry! I'm sorry!" I held his head between my hands. "I didn't mean it. It's been the worst day in the world."

One of the best things about Ansel is that he believes you when you say you're sorry. He doesn't make you wait or prove it, he just lets you start over and try again. He licked my face.

"Come on," I said. "Get the *leash*?"

That word lifted him right off the bed and down the stairs ahead of me. I had one last photo to shoot for the contest. It was "Your Name." I had planned to let Nate choose how we wrote his name, but he wasn't here. And even though I was hurt that he'd left, I still cared about Grandma Lilah seeing the loons. She might not remember it forever, but I would.

"I'm just taking Ansel for a quick walk. I'll be back," I yelled at the kitchen and hurried outside so Mom wouldn't say she'd come with us or see my face and ask me if something was wrong.

In the woods behind our house, Ansel sniffed each plant and rock he could reach on his leash. I followed behind him, from smelling place to smelling place, and gathered up long pinecones. Then I laid them out on a patch of ground to spell out NATE BAILEY.

After I shot a few photos of his name, I kicked and threw the pinecones in all different directions to erase the letters. Ansel thought it was a game and tried to chase after the pinecones. I let him bring one home in his mouth. It made the walk home shorter, because he couldn't smell things and carry a pinecone in his mouth at the same time.

Back in my room, Ansel shredded the pinecone to little bits on my rug, and I got out the contest list. I'd always imagined that Nate and I would make the final choices together, but as I looked at the photos and made decisions, I stopped minding he wasn't there and started feeling happy with the photos I had taken. With each photo, I asked myself if it was my best shot for that word. And then I considered if Dad might recognize it. But he'd spent so little time here before his trip; I didn't think anything in my photos would stand out to him. He might recognize Grandma Lilah when he met her again, but Dad had said he needed to pick the contest winner as soon as he got home. It was unlikely that he'd see her up close before then.

Beside each contest word was a space for a short comment. I wrote my descriptions as if Nate were writing them.

YOUR NAME: Nate Bailey.

DESIGN: The loon's back has a beautiful polka-dot pattern, and he has stripes on his neck.

THREE FEET: Friends at the lake.

SECRET: A great blue heron in the mist.

COLLECTION: Rock candy.

SKIP: Skimming rocks.

HOLDING ON: My grandmother's hand on the arm of a rocking chair.

STICKY: Melting banana split.

JOURNEY: Going down this mountain trail is a lot easier than climbing up.

BEYOND REACH: The mountains.

HEADING HOME: From the middle of the lake, looking back at our cottage.

AT THE SHORE: Loons can't walk very far, so they need to lay their eggs at the shore.

EXIT: The doorway out of our grocery store.

LEFT BEHIND: My grandmother waiting for us to come back.

LINES: Birch trees and blue sky.

A CLOSER LOOK: This chipmunk came to check out our snacks. He came for a closer look and a closer taste.

WONDER: A hand on the surface of the lake. I wonder what's going on down there underwater?

UNEXPECTED: A purple dragonfly. I'd never seen one this color before.

ON ITS OWN: When you're alone on a mountaintop, you feel like you're the only person in the world.

A NEW DAY: Sunrise and a lawn chair left overnight on our dock.

AT THE CROSSROADS: You can take either path on this mountain trail to get around these big rocks, but both ways are steep.

OUT OF PLACE: A girl's feet on the beach of her new house. She was scared that first day because everything was new.

TEXTURE: This toad blends in so well with the tree trunk that my friend and I almost didn't see him.

I looked at my two best "Lost" photos. The one of Grandma Lilah was honest. And the photo of Nate pretending to be lost in the woods — it just looked fake. I picked up my cell phone. *Please be there, Dad.*

"Hello?"

Relief washed through me. "Dad, I have a photography question."

"I'm in the middle of a shoot, but I'm glad you called. I'm sorry I hurt your feelings about the loon chick this morning."

"Thank you." It felt so nice to hear the concern in his voice. "I need help deciding something."

"What is it?" Dad asked.

"Let's say you took a great photo, but it was of a person, and someone in her family didn't like the way she looked in the photo."

"Well, people almost never like the way they look in photos. What the camera shows isn't always how they see themselves. They look heavier than they want or —"

"But what if it's for an article you're doing? And something good might come out of it? Would you use it?"

I heard him exhale, considering. "Did the person in the photo tell you it was okay to take their photo?"

"Yes."

"Well, I'd have to weigh the effect the photo could have on that one person against the bigger story. Maybe the photo is art? Or news? Or it's a photo that will change people's minds about something important. Important things are always complicated, and that's what makes them hard. But it's also what makes them matter."

"What if there's more than *one* thing that's important?"

"I don't know, Lucy. At some point, you just have to choose. And then be brave enough to stand up to the people who think you made the wrong choice."

I swallowed to keep my voice from breaking. "I miss you."

"Me, too. Only a little while longer, okay? We'll talk about everything you want to then."

"Okay," I said.

She doesn't remember, I wrote in the contest entry box.

A walk to the post office was a set number of steps — past the church, past the grocery store, past the gift shop, up the stairs, and into the building. I knew I could change my mind anytime until those last few seconds when I handed my envelope to the postmaster and paid the postage.

As I got to town, I felt my feet slowing down. *Am I holding back because this is a bad idea or just because I'm scared?*

I had always planned that Nate and I would mail our entry together, but he was off with Megan and I didn't want to talk about the pictures with him. If he asked which photo I had used for "Lost," I'd have to admit I'd used the one he didn't want me to.

Looking around Main Street, I realized this town already felt a tiny bit mine. Passing the grocery store, I wondered if I'd ever go in Barton's and not look for the EXIT sign and remember how Grandma Lilah couldn't find it. At the gift shop, I could see Emily's loon poster in the window: TAKE CARE OF THE LOONS BEFORE THEY'RE GONE FOREVER!

176

It's hard to think of anything being gone forever. Most things that go come back again, even if they're a little different when they return. But not always, and when something has gone forever, it can hurt so much you start wondering if it would've been easier if you'd never had it all.

Did I really wish that second chick had never hatched? Just because we didn't have him very long? Looking at the poster, I thought, *Maybe we can't solve every big problem, but we can try to solve the ones we can.*

Good things matter, even when they don't last forever. I couldn't bring back the loon chick or that day Nate and Grandma Lilah had climbed Cherry Mountain or any of the big things Grandma Lilah had lost, but maybe I could bring back a little thing.

Even if it wasn't exactly the way it used to be.

Even if it was just for an afternoon.

I might not win the contest money and take Grandma Lilah on Loon Patrol, but I walked faster — past the gift shop, up the post office steps, and through the door.

Even half a chance beats none.

19

Unexpected

For two weeks, I checked the mail every day, expecting a huge package of portfolios to arrive from the magazine sponsoring the contest. But not a single package came for Dad.

It felt like a big, heavy lump inside me not to tell Nate that I'd used the photo of Grandma Lilah for "Lost." On my walk home from the post office after mailing our entry, I had texted him, Our contest entry is in the mail. I hope we win.

My phone had chimed before I got home. I'm sorry

I didn't help. I just had 2 get away from home 4 a while. It's hard 2 keep pretending nothing happened.

Okay, I thought. *I can see that*. I had thought his deciding to go with Megan was about me, but he just needed a break. Have fun, I typed, and meant it.

As August moved on, the summer was slipping through my fingers. The sun set a little earlier each day, marking one day closer to Dad coming home but also one day less that Nate would be here. One day closer to everything changing.

Mom kept suggesting we go school shopping, but I didn't know what kind of clothes the kids wore here. She said the best things might be gone if we waited until school started, so finally I gave in and went to a mall with her. It was fun to have lunch and ice cream with Mom, and while I was there, I bought a scrapbook for photos. If we didn't win the contest, at least I could give Grandma Lilah copies of the loon photos that I had taken.

But it was hard to be with all those excited kids at the mall, heading back to friends and sports and clubs. I picked out a few new things to make Mom happy, but when I couldn't find any shoes I liked, I asked her if we could order them online instead.

"We have to register you for school," Mom said over breakfast one morning after I came back from checking the mail. *Where were those portfolios? They should be here by now.*

"I was thinking after breakfast I could call and see if the school office is open. Maybe the secretary can tell us where your classrooms will be and who your teachers are. She might even be able to show us your homeroom. Wouldn't that be nice?"

The idea of walking down empty hallways with some stranger telling Mom how great it all was and how much I'd like it there made me sick inside.

"I wanted to go on Loon Patrol," I said softly. "I don't have many chances left to go this year."

She looked a little disappointed, but she went without me and let me stay home.

At ten o'clock when I was leaving for Loon Patrol, Ansel looked so sad to be left behind that I gave in to those heartbreaking eyes. "I don't think you'll like it," I said, clipping on his leash. "It involves *water*. But if you hate it, I'll take you back to shore and stay with you."

On the dock, Nate and Emily were both surprised to see Ansel with me. "Do you know if he can swim?" Nate asked.

"Mrs. Rigby's dog has her own life vest," Emily said. "It has a handle on the back, so if her dog falls overboard, she can hoist her back in. Ansel looks about the same size as Zoe. I'll go see if I can borrow it."

"Zoe's vest is *pink*," Nate said, wrinkling his nose.

"Ansel's a dog!" Emily said. "He doesn't care if it's pink!"

But he cared about water. As she left, Ansel and I both looked doubtfully at the kayak. "Just remember, you were the one begging to come," I told him.

The pink doggy life preserver was a little too big, but it fit well enough to try it. "Would you hold Ansel while I get in the kayak, and then pass him to me?" I asked Emily as I adjusted the straps.

Emily picked up Ansel and held him on her hip, like he was a toddler. "You'll like it, Ansel. You'll see."

But when she waded into the water, Ansel waved his legs frantically. I got into the kayak as fast as I could and laid the paddle across the front.

"It'll be fun, Ansel!" Emily said, putting him in my arms.

I held on tight as Ansel's claws dug into my arm and his head rammed backward into my neck. Emily gave my kayak a big push and my paddle fell off the front of the kayak into the water. "Don't be scared," I whispered into Ansel's neck. "It was scary for me at first, too. But I won't let anything bad happen to you. I promise."

Nate moved his kayak up beside me and held out my paddle. "Can I help?"

Ansel was still shaking, but he wasn't trying to get down — probably because the only place to get down was into the lake. I kept one arm around him and reached for my paddle with my other. "You guys go on ahead. This might take awhile."

Ansel leaned back as tight against me as he could. But as we floated, I found I could let go of him enough to allow me to take a few strokes. I moved the kayak slowly through the water. "See? This isn't so bad."

By the time we passed Mrs. Rigby's house and Ansel saw her dog outside, he was comfortable enough to give some excited woofs — though he was still quivering. On the lake, his barks echoed. "They'll hear you all the way in Massachusetts!" I teased him.

"That would make a fun photo of the two of you," Nate said. "Do you have your camera?"

"No, I left it home. I figured I'd have my hands full with Ansel."

Nate nodded. "The contest was fun, but it's nice

having it done. We get to do things and see things without thinking about whether it's a good picture."

I smiled, but I couldn't help framing with my eyes all the shots I was missing. As we paddled around, Ansel fell asleep in my lap. I moved slowly and rhythmically, *dip and pull*.

"We've worn him out," Emily said.

"He's too tired to be scared now," I said. "I didn't think about it, but I'm not sure how I'll get *out* of the kayak with him."

"I'll go in first," Nate said. "Then I'll hop out and take him from you."

Going through the lily pads, I disturbed some insects hanging out there, and one shimmery-winged bug jumped onto the nose of my kayak. The need to save each moment was so strong in me that if I had my camera, I know I would've shot the scene. But instead, I let him walk onto my finger and deposited him on another lily pad.

Looking ahead to the dock, I saw Grandma Lilah standing there with her clipboard, waiting for us. My gaze wandered past her. Mom's car was back in our driveway. She was home from registering me at school. But when I glanced at our house, I startled so sharply that I woke Ansel.

Dad was on the porch.

20

On Its Own

"Hey!" Dad held out his arms to me as I raced up our front-porch steps. "Where were you? I missed you being here to greet me."

I hugged him as hard as I could. "I wouldn't have gone on Loon Patrol if I'd known you were coming home today. You weren't supposed to come home until Wednesday!"

"I thought I'd surprise you. I met some nice people on the plane and they gave me a ride from the airport to their house in Conway. Then when I called Mom to come get me, she was at your new school."

I couldn't believe he was here!

Ansel was jumping against Dad's leg, trying to lick his hand. "I saw you in the kayak, Ansel!" Dad reached down to stroke his ears. "Lucy has turned you into a real New Hampshire dog while I was away."

"He didn't like it at first, but then he went to sleep," I said. "So either he got comfortable with it, or he just got tired of worrying about it!"

"You looked great, Lucy. I loved seeing you both out there on the lake."

I grinned. "Do you want to see the loons? They were down by the point a few minutes ago. They might still be there. The baby is getting so big! He was black when he was tiny, but now he's more brown."

"Let's do it later," Dad said. "I haven't even unpacked yet. I have a million details to sew up from this trip — including that I lost a piece of luggage. Well, I didn't lose it, the airline did! And I have to call my editor. Somehow I have to tell Marjorie that my photos aren't exactly what we talked about."

"Okay." I tried not to let my disappointment show. The loons would be there later. "So, um, remember how you asked me to keep an eye out for a big package of kids' portfolios? They haven't come yet."

"Oh, I'm sorry. I forgot to tell you that you didn't have to watch for them anymore."

"What?" I stopped breathing. "Why?"

"When I told Marjorie I didn't think I'd have time, she picked ten finalists and made me an online gallery of their portfolios so I wouldn't have to weed through hundreds — only ten. She sent me the link a few days ago."

I let my breath go in a rush. "Marjorie picked the finalists? But that wasn't part of the rules. *You* were supposed to see all the entries and choose."

"Don't worry. I'm sure Marjorie knows what's okay. Thanks for reminding me, though. I have to pick the winner before I talk to her, because it's the first thing she'll ask me."

"Maybe you should choose the winner *now*?" I said. "Just think of those poor kids waiting and worrying and wondering and *waiting*."

"He's only just got home," Mom said through the screen door. "Give the poor man a minute."

Dad sighed. "You know, it *would* be nice to have that contest behind me. And maybe telling her I've picked the winner will soften the blow that I didn't exactly stick to my assignment. Okay. Do you want to help me choose, Lucy?"

"You choose first," I said. "Because you're the real judge." For once, I was glad he was so into his work. I wouldn't have to wait to find out.

Usually it seems so quick to walk into a house and boot up a laptop, but today it felt like forever.

When I imagined this moment, I thought I'd feel happy and excited, ready to say, "Look! I told you I was good at this."

I hadn't imagined that I'd feel so scared. I sucked in my bottom lip, to keep from saying anything and giving away how important this was to me.

"Okay, here's the list." Dad turned his laptop around, and I looked at the ten names. I didn't have to look far, because "Bailey" was right at the top.

I couldn't bear to sit next to Dad. It was too hard pretending I was only curious, not dying to know. He started scrolling through images, making "hmm" sounds.

"I'll be right back," I said. "I need some paper and a pen so I can take notes when it's my turn." But really, I hurried upstairs to get my camera so I could prove to him the photos from the contest were mine.

As soon as I won.

21

Beyond Reach

As Dad looked through the portfolio entries on his computer, I sat on our living room couch across from him and pretended to read a brochure on rare Arizona plants that he'd brought back from his trip. But my mind was too full of my own words.

Skip.

Journey.

Lost.

"Hmm," Dad murmured.

He couldn't be looking at my portfolio. When he saw the photo of Grandma Lilah, he wouldn't just say "hmm." He'd start talking and talking, like he does when he sees a photo that's so good he wishes he'd taken it.

With every moment that didn't happen, I felt like I was being put in my place. And it wasn't first. "Bailey" was at the top of the list of names; surely he'd seen my photos by now.

It hurt inside my chest. *Maybe I should've tried harder.* But even as I thought that, I knew I had done my best.

Maybe the answer was no.

Not good enough.

Not you.

"Okay," Dad said. "I've chosen. One portfolio stood out. It was an easy choice."

My throat was so tight that I could barely ask, "Who won?"

"Um, let's see. I picked Lucas from Oklahoma," Dad said. "He has a good eye. Okay, Lucy. Now you look at the portfolios and tell me which one you would've picked."

Dad brought me his laptop. On the screen was a photo of a barbed-wire fence against a storm-threatening sky. On the other side of the fence stretched a blurred flat prairie. But in the foreground, in sharp focus, were a few bursts of barbed-wire prickles and holding the wire was an older man's dirty, weathered hand, every wrinkle of his knuckles showing.

The top third of the photo was empty, just gray-green sky with one lonely, miserable line of barbed wire cutting across it. It felt like there was nowhere to go — even if you looked up, there was that line of prickled wire. It made me feel even more trapped.

"Is this one of the winner's photos?" I asked quietly.

Dad nodded. "This is 'beyond reach.' That was a hard one, because how do you show 'reach' in a photo? A photo is just a second of time, and Lucas shows it with this one lonely hand. It would've been easy for him to just shoot the fence, but the hand brings the story. It's great that he thought of that. All of the other kids just did things that were far away."

I put my camera back in my pocket, thinking of my photo of the mountains. "But aren't faraway things beyond reach?"

"Yeah, but 'beyond reach' means you *want* to reach something. It's more than far away; there's an absence. Missing something you can't have. There's nothing missing in the other photos. They're beautiful but they don't make me think about wanting what I can't have. Lucas shot 'beyond reach,' and all the other pictures are scenic views, and that's all."

That's all. Two little words as full of prickles as the barbed wire in the photo on Dad's laptop screen.

And the worst part was I knew he was right. I wanted so badly to win, but even *I* would choose this photo over mine.

I didn't want to see any more of that boy's photos, but Dad moved to the next one. "This is 'at the crossroads.'"

It was a black-and-white photo of a railway station, but Lucas must've sat or lay on the train tracks to take the photo, because the perspective was low and the tracks loomed huge in the foreground with the industrial-looking buildings and electrical wires and telephone poles softly blurred in the background.

"It was a smart choice to shoot this in black-and-white," Dad said. "What's great here are the different tones and textures that the black-and-white shows. And there's a good balance between the whitest whites and the blackest blacks. The things you want highlighted, like the tops of the train tracks, stand out because they are in the whitest white."

I wasn't sure I understood, but I tried to take it in. "I didn't think of using black-and-white," I said, but then quickly added, "I mean, I *wouldn't* think of using it."

Dad didn't notice my slipup, though. He was so into the photo.

"It's not a perfect photo," Dad said. "The background is too bright. It should be darker, because the photo is about the tracks, but the brightness of the background leads your eye up to there. You want to figure it out, but you can't because it's blurry. So he makes you look there, but there's no real payoff. If he had made this darker it would've been a better photo. I almost want to open up my photo editing program and fix it, because it's a good image, but it could be great."

"Are all his other photos as good as these?" I asked.

"Most are," he said. "Not every photo can be amazing, but he had several photos that took my breath away. Most of the other portfolios are good, but they're safe. Of course, that's what I'd expect from kids. It's hard to —"

"Then I'd choose him, too," I said flatly, wanting this to be over.

"You don't want to see the others?" Dad asked.

I shook my head. I needed some time to feel bad. There would be no prize money. No showing Dad my talent. No way to take Grandma Lilah out to see the loons. Summer would just *end*.

"Okay, then. Give me a few minutes here. I need to get my equipment out of the car and send a few things to Marjorie. Then maybe we can go see the loons?"

"I'm sure they've gone now," I said.

Heading upstairs to my room, I heard him open the porch door. "Hello! Beautiful day today!" he called to someone.

I didn't realize the trouble until I glanced out my window to see Nate and Grandma Lilah in their yard. And to my horror, Grandma Lilah started walking right over to Dad as he took his suitcase out of our car.

Wait! He can't meet her up close yet! What if he recognizes her? I ran down the stairs, but as I got to the front porch, Dad, Nate, and Grandma Lilah were already talking. "Such a lovely girl, our Lucy of the Loons," Grandma said as I rushed up beside Dad.

He grinned. "Lucy has really enjoyed *your* family."

"It's time for Loon Patrol," Grandma Lilah said.

"We've already done it today," Nate said. "The loons were down near the point."

"And the babies?" she asked.

"They're getting big," Nate said.

"I must write that down!" she said, turning for the house.

Nate sighed. "Sorry. She's mixed up today. She's having a hard time remembering things. It's nice to meet you, Mr. Emery."

"Remembering things?" Dad's forehead tensed. "Nate? Are you a photographer?"

My mouth was completely dry as Nate looked at me. I shook my head at him, but Dad said, "Nate Bailey! From the kids' photography contest, right?"

"Sorry, you didn't win, Nate!" I said quickly. "Some kid from Oklahoma did."

"Lucy! You're not supposed to tell him! Marjorie will be mad at me." Dad laughed. "So *this* is why you were so interested in the contest entries, Lucy."

I didn't know what to say, but Dad had already turned back to Nate. "I probably shouldn't say anything, but you're a runner-up," Dad told him. "When I started reviewing the portfolios, I didn't expect to see a photo I wished I'd taken myself. But I felt that way about one of yours, Nate. In fact, I awarded it best photo. It's a brave image."

"Brave?" Nate asked.

Dad inclined his head toward Grandma Lilah on the porch, looking for the clipboard. "The photo for 'lost' showing your grandmother," Dad said quietly. "It stays with me. A good photo can do that. It can make someone care."

Nate's eyes flashed to mine. "You used it? After what I said?"

My throat felt so full I could barely talk. "I wanted to —"

But Nate turned and ran away from me. He stormed past Grandma Lilah looking for her clipboard on their porch and into their cottage, slamming the screen door behind him.

"What was that about?" Dad asked.

"I have something to tell you," I said slowly. I wasn't used to making such big mistakes. "Those photos weren't really Nate's. I mean, he helped, but he didn't actually take them."

"So who shot the photos?" Dad asked.

I couldn't believe he didn't see it. I looked into his eyes.

"Me," I said.

22

At the Crossroads

At home, Dad had barely touched the sandwich Mom had set on the kitchen table in front of him. "Lucy, why did you do this?" he asked. "Now there are only nine finalists, and Marjorie will have to go back through all those portfolios and choose another one."

"But why? If my photo won, then —"

"I can't choose you as a runner-up! People will think I picked you because you're my daughter!"

I couldn't help the tears in my eyes. But inside, I was really mad, too. He was upset with me because it might make *him* look bad. "I'm a finalist because my photos were good enough," I said flatly. "But you wouldn't have seen that if my name was on them."

Dad stared. "So you did this to prove something to *me*?"

"Maybe at first I wanted that a little. But there's something I want even more now." I could feel a tear crawling down the side of my nose, but I left it there. "I want to win the prize money to rent a pontoon boat to get Grandma Lilah out to see the loons."

"A *pontoon* boat?" Mom asked.

"Because motorized rafts cost too much," I said, "and she can't climb into a regular boat or a kayak, so all she can do is watch the loons from the dock. And they don't swim over on our side of the lake a lot because of all the people. Maybe this is Grandma Lilah's last summer here."

Now that I'd said it out loud, it sounded ridiculous. How could renting a pontoon boat ever make a difference? Grandma Lilah's problems were bigger, more impossible than that.

"Oh, Lucy," Mom said quietly. "You can't do the wrong thing, even for the right reasons."

Dad sighed. "I love that you care so much about the family next door. Maybe next summer we can —"

"No!" I said. "You always promise me things for

later. But maybe this time there aren't more chances." I took a deep breath and looked right at him. "It's the magazine's contest. They should decide if it's okay."

Dad dropped his head back to stare at the ceiling. "You're putting me in a hard position, Lucy."

"If Marjorie says yes, that photo will go in the magazine," Mom said. "That may not be the kind of attention the Baileys want to have, Lucy. If Marjorie agrees to this, you have to ask Grandma Lilah and her family and let them decide."

I hadn't thought of how public winning would be. I looked out the window to our driveway. Could I go to the Baileys and tell them? Nate was already mad at me. What would the rest of them think when they saw the photo? Would it hurt them to see it? They had been so nice to me all summer.

But the runner-up prize was enough money for a whole day's rental of a pontoon boat. It felt even worse to think of the Baileys leaving when I hadn't even tried.

"Ask Marjorie," I said. "While you call her, I have something I need to finish."

"Good afternoon," Grandma Lilah said from her porch chair. "You just missed Nate."

"Come inside, Grandma Lilah!" I heard Nate yell from inside the cottage.

"Oh, there you are, Nate! We have company!" Grandma Lilah called to him. "Lucy and her dad are here."

Standing on her cottage porch holding my scrapbook, I wanted to cry, but I knew it'd worry her. "I came to see you, Grandma Lilah. But first I have to give Nate something. I'll be right back, okay?"

Dad leaned against the porch railing and started talking about how beautiful the lake looked and how nice it was to be home.

Inside the cottage, I couldn't even look at Nate on the couch by himself. "I made this scrapbook for Grandma Lilah," I said quietly so she wouldn't have any chance of hearing me out on the porch. "I put in some of my photos from the contest, but also a lot of the regular photos I took this summer. I thought she might like to have them."

I held the scrapbook out to him, but Nate didn't take it. "Megan said it was okay for me to use the photos she took of the loon babies, too."

His eyes opened a little wider. He was probably surprised by that, but not as shocked as Megan had looked to find me on her cottage steps yesterday. She had crossed her arms over her stomach. Maybe she thought I was bragging as I told her my idea about the scrapbook. Then I said, "And I wanted to ask if I could make copies of the photos you took of the two babies. I don't have any good close-ups of the two little loons together, and you took some great ones."

Megan's mouth had dropped open, but when she came back with her camera, she said, "I'm sorry I deleted your photos. The first one was an accident, but then I kept going."

I nodded. "I'm sorry we had a bad start this year."

"There's always next year," she said, and I saw a little bit of friendliness in her eyes.

"Yeah," I'd said.

But standing in Nate's cottage, I could hear Grandma Lilah out on the porch, laughing at something Dad had said. And I knew that next year might be really different in some ways. "You can decide when to give it to her, okay? I don't want to mess things up like I did at the cookout." I left it on a little table near the door. "Whenever you think is good."

Out on the porch, I sucked my bottom lip, waiting for a pause in Dad's conversation with Grandma Lilah about the hanging baskets on her porch. "Grandma Lilah, I have to tell you something," I said.

Dad put his hand on my shoulder. It felt solid and

nice there. I hadn't expected him to come with me, but I was so glad that he had. He made me feel braver.

"A few weeks ago, you and I were sitting here on the porch and I had my camera," I said to Grandma Lilah. "We were waiting for the other kids to come back from Loon Patrol, and I was fooling around taking photos for my photography contest. You showed me your Doris Day movie star look."

Grandma Lilah smiled. "She was my favorite!"

But I was fighting the urge to throw up. "One photo was different than the others. You looked worried in that one."

"Worried?"

"I should've asked you if it was okay to show it to people. But I didn't do that. I sent it to the photography contest. I just kept thinking what a good photo it was. If we won, Nate and I wanted to use the money to get you out on the lake to see the loons. I guess I thought if I were doing it for a good reason, that made it okay."

She held out her hand. "Let me see."

See what?

"Let me see the photo," she said.

"You don't want to see it," I heard Nate say from inside the house.

"Of course I do!" Grandma Lilah said.

She didn't put her hand down, so I took my camera out of my pocket and scrolled backward to the photo of her sitting up very straight in the porch rocking chair, holding the teacup in her hands, her eyes full of panic. I held my breath, handing my camera to her. "I'm sorry."

"What happened?" she asked, looking at it.

I didn't know how much to tell her. "I gave you the teacup to hold and you said it wasn't yours. You got upset, until I said it was mine."

"I'm not well," Grandma Lilah said softly.

"Don't say that," Nate said. I looked over to see him standing on the other side of the screen door.

"But if I can't say it, I have to go through it alone." Grandma Lilah held the camera closer to look carefully at the screen. "My eyes look scared."

"I know," I said, dropping my gaze to the porch floorboards. "I shouldn't —"

"But my hair looks wonderful."

I glanced up, surprised to see her smiling. "Did it win the contest?"

"Runner-up," I said.

"*Maybe* runner-up," Dad said. "Just because my editor said yes doesn't mean it's decided. Grandma Lilah, if Lucy wins, this photo will go in a magazine. Lots of people will see it. You and your family need to decide if that's okay with you. And I have to decide if it's okay with me that my daughter entered. I'm the judge."

"Well, it's not *your* picture," Grandma Lilah said.

"No," Dad said. "But people might think —"

"Oh, people will think what they think!" Grandma Lilah said. "Don't ever choose the people who don't matter over the ones who do."

I didn't know that you could choke on air, but Dad did.

"I've never had my photo in a magazine," Grandma Lilah said. "Have I, Nate?"

"No." He opened the screen door. "At least I don't think so."

She laughed. "I'll be just like Doris Day. She was in all the magazines."

I hadn't noticed the scrapbook in Nate's hand until he laid it in her lap. "Lucy made this for you."

"For me? Oh, thank you, dear." Turning the pages, she smiled at the photos of the loons, the view at the top of Cherry Mountain, Nate skipping the rock, and the photo he took of me in the kayak.

Underneath my photo, I'd written "Lucy of the Loons."

"So you'll remember me," I said.

"I can't promise that," she replied softly as she turned the pages.

23

A Closer Look

The next day, I walked over to join Nate and Emily and Grandma Lilah on the dock for Loon Patrol.

Nate didn't look up as he filled out the form for today's weather and lake conditions. We hadn't really made up, and it didn't look like we were about to.

"We can't go yet," I said. "We have to wait."

"Why?" Emily asked. "Did you forget something?"

"Nope." I couldn't help grinning. "But Grandma Lilah needs to put on sunscreen and get her binoculars and maybe bring a sweater. It might be windy in the middle of the lake."

That made Nate look up from the form.

I pointed down the shore to the pontoon boat heading our way. Dad was driving and Mom held on to Ansel's collar as he stood on the seats, barking to see me.

"My parents loaned me the prize money ahead, and we've rented this for the whole day," I said. "So, Grandma Lilah, you're coming on Loon Patrol. In fact, you can go out on the lake as many times as you want today."

Emily clasped her hands together. "What a great idea, Lucy!"

Nate gave a small smile, handing Grandma Lilah the clipboard. "We'll need this."

"Dad said we have enough room for eight people," I said. "So we can all go this time and we have room for two more. Everyone else can take turns."

"I'll go get my parents!" Emily said, taking off for the cottage. "And I'll grab your binoculars and a sweater, Grandma Lilah."

"A boat ride? Oh, how nice!" she said, like it was something that might happen any day.

On the other hand, Mr. and Mrs. Bailey looked *very* surprised to see a pontoon boat tied up at their dock as they came down the lawn toward the beach a few minutes later. But they seemed even more shocked to see Grandma Lilah sitting in one of the forward seats.

"Hurry up or you'll miss the boat!" Grandma Lilah laughed at her own joke.

"Grandma Lilah, do you want to sit back here under the canopy?" Dad asked. "You'd be out of the sun and you wouldn't get any spray."

"No," she said. "I want to be right here where the action is!"

Nate, Grandma Lilah, Emily, Ansel, and I sat on the pontoon boat's two long vinyl-cushioned benches facing each other at the front. Next to me, there was a sink and a little refrigerator. In the middle of the boat, Dad sat at the wheel. Beside him and behind him, Mom and the Baileys spread out on more rows of seats.

"Morgan and Mason will be mad that they went to town with Aunt Pat and missed this," Emily said, across from me.

"We have the boat all day," I said. "So they can have a turn this afternoon. I want to ask someone else, too."

Megan and I might not ever be good friends, or even just good summer friends, but when we got back, I was going to walk over to her cottage and invite her. Because maybe we both wanted to try, and sometimes people are like shooting photos. It takes a bunch of misses before something good happens.

Dad started the boat, and I could smell the fuel as he backed up. Then he turned the bow toward open water and I leaned against the seat, listening to the low rumble of the engine as we cut slowly across the lake.

"It's like a floating living room!" Grandma Lilah called over the sound of the engine. "Can we go faster?"

Dad nodded. "You bet!" As he increased the speed, spray flew off the sides and our wake fanned out behind us. I reached my arm over the side, trying to touch the water droplets jumping into the air.

"Ansel likes this better than kayaking," I said to Nate, hoping he'd say something back, but he just stared out over the water.

Out in the middle, the wind was stronger, sweeping my hair across my nose every time I turned my head. I faced forward again to get my hair back to the sides. People were talking, but Grandma Lilah was looking ahead. "Can we go over there?" she asked, pointing to the cove where the loons had built their nest.

"We can go anywhere you want," Dad said.

I took a few photos for Nate to add to Grandma Lilah's scrapbook, but then I put my camera away. It was hard not to capture everything, but after a little while, something amazing happened. I simply saw it. Not to share. Not to capture. Just to live what was around me.

"The wind makes you feel completely alive, doesn't it?" Grandma Lilah asked, smiling.

Nate leaned across to whisper something to me. I tipped my head toward him and braced myself in case he was still mad.

"Thanks for this," he said. "She's having a great time."

"Nate, I'm sorry," I said.

"I don't like to think about her getting worse," he said close to my ear. "I'm afraid she'll forget *me* someday."

I opened my mouth to tell him it'd all be okay, but I didn't know what would happen. And neither did he.

"She remembers today," I whispered.

He nodded. "Today, she does."

In the cove, the water looked greener. As we moved, the clouds reflected in the surface of the lake appeared to be moving, too, racing with the spray off the sides of our boat. We saw a great blue heron, a Canada goose, and lots of ducks. "Where are our loons?" Grandma Lilah asked.

I didn't know what would happen when Grandma Lilah only saw one little loon. But I planned to go along with anything Nate told her.

Dad slowed the boat until we were only floating. Waves echoed under the boat. "Does anyone see them?" he asked.

And there they were: a trio of dark heads above the water.

"Oh, they're so beautiful," Grandma Lilah said. "And there's one of the babies! Where's the other one? Does anyone see it?"

I waited for Nate to say the second chick was hiding or diving, but he leaned toward her. "Grandma Lilah, something sad happened, and there's only one chick now."

It felt like my heart stopped beating as Grandma Lilah said, "No, we have *two* this year. We wrote it down."

"There *were* two," Nate said gently. "But a bald eagle came, and he took one."

"An eagle!" Grandma Lilah put her hand to her throat. "That can't be right. We've never had eagles on the lake."

"I know," Nate said. "But we had one this year. Lucy saw him."

"Our poor baby!" Grandma Lilah's eyes filled with tears.

I swallowed hard. This boat trip was supposed to make her happy, not make her cry. "I'm so sorry," I said. "The loons tried really hard. They dove and dove, and I tried to scare the eagle, but he didn't give up."

"I've never seen an eagle in real life, only in pictures. Was he beautiful?" she asked.

Beautiful? I looked in her eyes, still wet with tears. The eagle had done something so awful that I hadn't seen anything else. Was he beautiful? "I guess so. He was horrible and beautiful together."

She nodded, wiping her eye with the side of her finger. "Write that down, Nate."

"I will." As Nate filled out the survey form, Dad steered the boat deeper into the cove. The male loon swam in the water on one side of the boat, the female and Baby One on the other. They didn't seem at all upset that we were there, but they called to each other, checking in.

"They're saying hello to you," I said to Grandma Lilah.

She shook her head. "They're telling me good-bye."

I opened my mouth to say no, but she stopped me. "Good-bye isn't the worst thing in the world. Sometimes it's simply time to go."

We stayed there a long time, just floating, watching the loons diving. Every time they popped up again, Grandma Lilah smiled. "There they are! Do you see them?"

"I can get us a little closer, but not closer than one hundred fifty feet," Dad said. "I saw that on a poster at the marina."

I glanced over to find him grinning at me.

And my heart felt warm and full.

When we finally headed back to the dock, I was tired of sitting sideways. So I turned around and knelt on the seat, holding on to the rail. Nate slid his hand along the boat's rail until the side of his finger touched the side of mine. I expected him to move it, but he left it there.

"Do you remember when we climbed Cherry Mountain, and said how we wished we could freeze a day and keep it that day always?" he asked.

I nodded.

"This is my day," he said.

On the morning Nate left to go home for the winter, I stood in our driveway with Ansel in my arms and waved good-bye. I was trying to look happy, but my heart felt as empty as their cottage would be when their van drove away.

"Bye, Lucy!" Nate said through the open window. "I'll email and text you and stuff like that. Okay?"

"Sure," I said, though I knew when he got home, he'd be busy with his regular friends in his regular life.

"Bye, Lucy!" Morgan yelled.

"Bye, Ansel!" Mason added.

I picked up Ansel's paw and waved it to them. "Bye!"

"Lucy of the Loons," Grandma Lilah called out the window. "Don't forget me when you go."

I didn't tell her that she was the one leaving. And that I'd remember long after she did. "I'll keep track of the loons until you come back, Grandma Lilah."

"I've never been here in the fall to see them leave," she said. "Or seen them come back in the spring. They are always here when I arrive and they leave the lake after I've gone. Wish them a safe journey for me."

"I will," I promised, waving and waving as their van drove away.

24

Hope

At the end of October, after the red, orange, and yellow leaves had fallen and all the tourists had gone, it was so quiet you could hear the waves on the beach, even before you saw the lake. It was a nice sound, always there.

I leaned my brand-new bike against the side of Nate's empty cottage porch. All around the lake were reminders of summer people. Cottages had their shades down, like sleeping eyes. Wharves and docks had been pulled up on the lawns. Rowboats were upside down, tied to trees or snug against the sides of cottages. Nate's family's kayaks lay piled up under their porch.

Every afternoon when I got home from school, I'd checked for Baby One, always afraid he'd leave while I was gone and I'd miss saying good-bye.

And every time I heard him, I was relieved.

Still here.

It made me as happy as every time I turned on my phone and there was another text from Nate. He'd sent four today already.

I'm glad ur dad bought bikes. Can I borrow his next year? We can go on some trails.

Cafeteria food stinks. I wish they'd serve No Mores.

GL had the scrapbook open 2 ur photo 2day. How come summer takes so long 2 come back?

Is the little loon still there? It must be getting cold.

The late-day autumn sun was bright, throwing long shadows, but not strong enough to warm the air. As I headed for the lake, my own shadow stretched out over the sand: a small body with legs as long as a stilt-walker.

The lake looked different in the fall, too. The town had opened the dam wide to drop the water level to allow for next spring's melting. Suddenly there was new beach, soft and gooey with light-green pondweeds — the gucky things I touched on the bottom last summer. As I stepped closer, my foot stuck in the cold, squishy mud. I yanked it out, my footprint filling immediately with water.

Please still be here, Baby One. I knew he had to leave before the lake froze, but he didn't have to leave yet. Not today.

I turned on my camera zoom so I could use it to scan the lake for that dark head, his neck snakelike above the water. *There he was, out in the middle of the lake!* I let my breath go with relief.

His bill opened, calling, *I'm here. Where are you?*

But no answer came.

A few weeks ago, the two adult loons had taken to the sky, their wings flapping furiously as they circled the lake together.

"They're leaving!" I'd screamed to Baby One. "Go with them!"

But he just kept swimming, calling, as the adults flew off over the trees without him.

"Don't worry," the lady at the Loon Preservation Committee office had said when I called, barely able to get the words out to explain that he'd been left behind. "The adults often leave for the ocean first. The young loon is on his own now. In a few weeks, he'll go, too."

"But how will he know where to go?" I asked. "He's never been to the ocean before."

"We don't understand how they know," she said. "But they do."

This time, watching him through my camera, I knew something was different. He kept stretching his wings, over and over. Getting ready.

I could barely breathe as he started running on the water. Faster and faster his feet slapped the surface, his wings pumping.

I took one photo and then put my camera down, wanting to share our last seconds without anything between us. He took to the air, pumping his wings hard.

Leaving the water behind him, he circled the lake to gain speed. "Safe journey!" I called to him. "From Grandma Lilah and me."

And there was nothing but sky.

Tears slid down my face. Would he really know where to go? And even if he did, so many miles and dangers stood between him going to the sea and coming back to find his own territory one day. Would he make it?

Sometimes you don't get an answer, though. Sometimes "I hope so" is the only answer you get.

All the loons have gone, I texted Nate. Tell Grandma Lilah I wished them a safe journey for her. I'll let the LPC know.

But I couldn't push SEND. That would make it over. As I stood next to Nate's empty cottage, a whole winter stretched ahead. School was going okay and the kids had been nicer than I expected, especially a girl named Mattie from the other side of the lake who rode the bus with me. But just knowing I wouldn't hear the loons or see them again for months — or maybe ever — made me incredibly lonely.

I imagined Baby One in the sky, seeing the world as I'd seen it from the top of Cherry Mountain. Blue upon blue mountains ahead, a carpet of trees below, the long curling rivers between the lakes, and somewhere far ahead, that huge ocean.

It must take some courage to fly, to trust the wind to hold you as it lifts you away from all you've ever known. To know inside that you're heading where you're meant to go — even if you've never been there before.

And that "I hope so" will be enough to get you there.

I'm here. Where are you?

I typed, finishing my text, and pushed SEND. Turning toward home, I had barely walked my bike across our driveway when my phone chimed an answer.

Just two words. But all Nate needed to say.

I'm here.